THE
WILD
BEFORE

THE WILD BEFORE

PIERS TORDAY

Quercus

QUERCUS CHILDREN'S BOOKS

First published in Great Britain in 2021 by Hodder & Stoughton

1 3 5 7 9 10 8 6 4 2

A CIP catalogue record for this book
is available from the British Library.

HB ISBN 978 1 786 54111 6
Exclusive ISBN 978 1 786 54182 6
PB ISBN 978 1 784 29456 4

Typeset in Book Antiqua by Palimpsest Book Production Ltd, Falkirk, Stirlingshire
Printed and bound in Great Britain by Clays Ltd, Elcograf S.p.A.

The paper and board used in this book
are made from wood from responsible sources.

Quercus Children's Books
An imprint of
Hachette Children's Group
Part of Hodder & Stoughton Limited
Carmelite House
50 Victoria Embankment
London EC4Y 0DZ

An Hachette UK Company
www.hachette.co.uk

www.hachettechildrens.co.uk

To Laszlo, who hopes

The following takes place some years before
the events described in *The Last Wild*

Animals, as is well known, mark
what we call months by new moons.
Tradition ascribes each new moon
to a different beast.

Wolf Moon (January)

Crow Moon (February)

Worm Moon (March)

Swallow Moon (April)

Hare Moon (May)

Cow Moon (June)

ANIMAL TIME

Stag Moon (July)

Harvest Mouse Moon (August)

Owl Moon (September)

Fox Moon (October)

Badger Moon (November)

Robin Moon (December)

A
FIELD GUIDE
TO THE
ANIMAL TONGUE

animal – any living creature apart from humans

beyond – animal afterlife

breath – fog, mist or spray

call – a cry

dream – animal story or myth

dwelling – any animal home, from a barn to a sett

hare-way – secret path known only to hares

he-child – human boy

firestick – gun

fish-path – stream

fish-road – river

form – where hares sleep

Great Rock – a boulder at the centre of every wild, used for addressing animals *green* – grass

Guardians – animals chosen to protect the wild,
    often the strongest predator in the group

jack-hare – male hare

jill-hare – female hare

leveret – baby hare

magic – human science and technology

meuse – hare-made hole in hedge or fence

moon – animal version of a month, determined
    by a new moon

open – open land, such as a field or moor

she-child – human girl

stingers – nettles

tall-home – tree, home to many creatures

tongue – language

walkupon – path

wet – flood

white – snow

whiterforce – waterfall

wild – group of animals brought together
    by habitat, food source or shared need

Wildness – the leader of a wild, appointed
    by discussion.

THE HARE'S MESSAGE

LITTLE HARE HAS BEEN RUNNING FOR SO LONG.

His eyes are wild, and his whiskers frazzled. Thorns have jabbed at his weary legs, and dew soaks his tight belly. There has been barely a moment to rest or feed on his long journey over these barren hills, which is why his ribs now poke through his ragged fur. A glittering mist flies from his feet as he bounds over the marshy earth, a mist that has trailed him all the way.

Can't stop . . . don't stop . . . won't stop, he gasps, over and over, until he wonders whether he will ever stop again.

As he bounds over the wet green, he keeps twisting his head around, sniffing the wind, staring in terror. His long, black-tipped ears twitch in alarm, as they have since he left the valley of his birth, a whole moon ago.

Can't see it . . . can't smell it . . . can't hear it, he keeps reminding himself. But he knows it is coming, faster than any hare can run, and the thought of this drives him on, over highlands and moorlands, over hedges and ditches, as if he is trying to outrun the wind itself.

He runs until he worries his hare-heart, powerful as it is, might burst with exhaustion. Little-Hare hopes that will not happen, as he has only lived for two summers, and would like to see at least a couple more.

Here and there, as he lopes in swerving lines across the moors, he spies a sheaf of grasses or a clump of crispy, withered bracken, and imagines how sweet it would be to stop, scrabble a shallow form out of the earth behind them, and lie down, out of sight, and sleep.

But if you stop now, he thinks, leaping over a boggy puddle, you might never get up!

Besides, he has a promise to keep, one he must keep all on his own. His fath-hare and moth-hare have long crossed over to the Great Beyond, and his sist-hare . . . is why he must keep his promise.

Little-Hare hopes he is racing the right way. He has never been this far north in the Island before. The weather is only ever strange these days, but grows worse the further he travels. And the land is so wide and bare, unlike the soft green valley of his home wild.

Dandelion Hill.

Even the name sounds warmer than here, he thinks,

as he runs under drizzly skies up marshy slopes. He has dreamed of little else on his journey. The wide opens of golden wheat, the soft ash, beech and oak tall-homes, and the high ridge overlooking all, with a view down to the ever-roaring fish-road.

Little-Hare remembers a grassy hillside bright with rain – and rolling down it with his sist-hare, frisking and fighting, batting her away with his forefeet. Or chasing butterflies in the wheat open, pelting through the stalks as fast as they could, trying to outrace each other – and how she was *always* bigger, stronger, faster.

They sat on the ridge together and watched the summer sun set, a honeysuckle light that sweetened the whole valley. They sheltered under willow boughs when the autumn sky wept tears and dug out the white in winter with frozen paws.

They skipped and gambolled. They touched noses and felt together.

Yes, that was Dandelion Hill, he remembers sadly. *That was *before*.*

And now Little-Hare's heart swells, only not from all the racing, but from a feeling of longing rising deep within that threatens to wash him clean away.

I mustn't! he thinks. Never!

He must not let it overwhelm him, ever again.

Got to run on.

Then, just as he feels he can run no further, what is this looming out of the marsh breath that rolls over the hilltop in front of him? The leaves and branches of some tall-homes! Just to see them in this empty land makes something quicken inside.

The calls and cries grow stronger here, and the scents too, so many beasts, some he does not recognise, not even from his long journey north. *Is this it?* he wonders. *Have I found them at last?*

For, to keep his promise, Little-Hare seeks a *wild*. In the language all beasts share, a group of creatures brought together by breeding, place or shared need, guided by their chosen leader, a *Wildness*.

This is the last wild he must reach with his message. Everywhere else he has tried, he has been . . . too late. His own wild lived on farmland, with all beasts united together, led by a—

Can't think about that. Block it out.

He shakes his head, blinking. He must not dwell on the past, he must focus on the message he carries, the news he has to deliver.

Little-Hare hopes for a friendly welcome at this new dwelling, as is traditional between wilds. There will be a Great Rock for addressing fellow creatures from, brave Guardians keeping the wild safe from unwanted intruders, secret shelters concealed under bushes in the deepest parts of the forest. Calls will be sung, dreams revealed, and lonely animal as he is, he will be together again, feel part of something bigger than him, all connected and tangled, joined through root and stem and cry.

The wild world.

If he was not so dizzy with tiredness, he would jump for joy.

I'm here, Run-Hare, he says to the voice inside his head, the voice that has not left him this whole time. *Like I promised. I made it.*

At least, that is what he hopes.

For what he arrives at is not the cosy tall-home wood of his daydream, full of sun-dappled walk-upons, cooing pigeons and chattering rooks. Instead, sombre, ancient oaks, taller and wider than he has ever seen before, rise out of the ground to block his way. Two wizened trunks stand out front, solid as gateposts.

It is winter. There are traces of white on the ground, and pretty patches of sow-bread flowers brightening the roots of the gateway tall-homes. He slinks to a halt and loiters just inside the edge of the old forest. Beyond, there are twisting roots, strands of cobweb stretching from bough to gloomy bough, with no other sign of life . . .

Apart from the eyes!

How could he miss them?

The three pairs of amber eyes, glowing in the shadows.

Little-Hare bobs up straight away, standing tall on his hind legs, to let these foxes know he has seen them. A signal which warns any hunter that even if they leaped for him now, he would beat them in a race. There is no faster animal across land on this island than a hare, even one as tired as he.

This plan might have worked, except that these watchers are not foxes. Slipping into the greyish light, these are animals whom the hare did not realise still lived in the further reaches of the Island. No wonder they have stayed hidden, in this faraway forest. But not so hidden now, with their stone-coloured fur and shining eyes, teeth bared as they circle him.

Wolves.

The hare doesn't know if he can outrun these new hunters, so he doesn't even try, and collapses into a crouch, ears flat, overtaken by an uncontrollable shiver.

What brings you to Stag Wood, stranger? growls one.

State your business, says another.

*And quick, for we are *hungry*,* adds the last.

The hare glances at each one in turn, taking in their size and strength.

My name is Little-Hare, small for my kind . . . he begins, and they snicker.

What a shame. I was hoping for more than a snack, murmurs the third, padding closer to sniff the cowering hare. His muzzle is starting to grey.

But Little-Hare has not come this far to be eaten so soon.

And I bring urgent news, from the wild of Dandelion Hill, in the south.

Very well, sneers the first wolf. *Tell us your news, and if it is interesting, we will give you a head start, before we rip you limb from limb.*

Little-Hare shakes his head. *I am under strict orders to speak to your Wildness only.*

8

He leaps back, a pair of jaws snapping in his face.

We are the Guardians of this wild! We decide who speaks to our Wildness! The second wolf is nearly upon him.

Little-Hare can feel her weight, her breath and heat, ready to consume him in an instant. For a moment, he feels death, a night-black smoke coiling around his paws, leaching into his fur, and he shudders.

At the same time, he remembers. He has seen death before. In fact, he and death know each other well, even if they are not exactly the best of friends. What are these wolves, compared to the wave of horror that follows fast behind him, that can outrun any hare or wolf, smothering them in one instant under its dark crest?

He looks up, his damp head trembling, to meet the wolf's eye. The Guardian pauses, puzzled. This is not typical hare behaviour. Hares should be wary and quick. This one is stubborn and sullen.

Get out of my way, says Little-Hare.

The wolf throws her head back, howling with laughter.

I'm sorry, what did you say?

I said, get out of my way.

The other wolves join in the laughter, shaking with mirth. They are too amused to even tear his soft belly open with their claws, as they were about to.

Give us one good reason why we should, says the first wolf.

Little-Hare is not laughing. His watchful amber eyes

never leave the wolves for a second. He sighs, and delivers the message that has been burning in his belly since he left the valley he called home.

*Because our world is about to end. There is nothing you wolves can do to stop the enemy chasing me. I was chosen, I tried, and . . . your wild is my last chance. *Our* last chance. So unless you want to die, get out of my way. Now.*

Then, before they can reply, he is off, bounding further and further into the deep oak wood.

For he is not just any hare.

He is the hare of all hope.

PART 1: DANDELION HILL

It hadn't always been like this, of course.

There was a before, and it was only eight moons ago. Swallow Moon.

A before of dandelions dancing down the slope, their golden faces catching the last rays of sun. Little-Hare sat on the ridge of the hill that swept down to Old Farm, his ears twitching as the clear skies faded away. His short shadow sank into a crack of earth.

Dandelion Hill was getting older. He tried not to think too much about that, or the fact the weather no longer behaved as it should.

I can't believe it's so cold still, he thought to himself.

Despite the chill in the air, spring had arrived in the valley, and the first swallows were returning, perching on the high human lines which criss-crossed the farmyard below as if they had never left. Buttery oxlips edged Ash Wood next to him, and skylarks hovered in song over the farm's endless wheat opens, where the first green tips of this year's feast already speared through the soil.

Each spring, the swallows were not the only new arrivals on the farmland. Little-Hare could also spy this season's woolly-headed lambs curled up, panting, on old mole hills, resting after a day of games and races. The cows were quiet, and the birds were preparing to sleep. And from a holly bush in Ash Wood, a robin put out his evening call. To the human ear, this sounded like a sweet melody, but to the animals of this wild it sounded just as it always did.

Right! Night-time! What are night-times for? Fighting! Who wants some? You looking at me, bird? Outside, now!

Behind Little-Hare, way up on the heathland, stood the stones of the Hare Circle, and ahead, in the distance, the ancient fish-road glinted as it wound its way through the valley, past Old Farm itself.

This, then, was their wild. Dandelion Hill. All the animals who lived on the farm, or made their home on the farmland around it, had the same Wildness, followed the same rules. Even as the farm itself changed more than any of them could have imagined.

Once, his fath-hare had said, there was just the old human dwelling, with smoke curling out of the stump on top. Around a bare yard, there had been a handful of beast dwellings: a traditional, old-fashioned farm.

But recently, under new ownership, the beast dwellings now dwarfed the human one, swollen into mighty structures of iron – shelter for hundreds of cows, sheep, pigs, goats and chickens. Every kind of animal a human could breed, feed . . . and eat. And dogs, he remembered with a shudder.

The hares tried to keep out of the way of the new people who lived there as much as they could. These humans hunted hares with their hounds, ate hares, and often put up fences where hares used to run, or sprayed opens with their magic breath, which made them poisonous. But through the other animals, they knew there was a farmer, and the farmer's mate, and a farmer's he-child and she-child, and plenty of farm workers.

They didn't know their names, or want to. Although, on every building, every vehicle, the back of every farm worker's overalls, there was one name repeated.

Facto, Little-Hare murmured to himself. Not a word he understood, just one he heard the humans use a lot.

FACTO – short for Factorium, the largest food company in the world.

But he would learn what it meant, in time. They would all learn.

Little-Hare washed his face, giving his velvety fur a good scratch with his paws. He turned to his sist-hare beside him, who was licking her forelegs clean.

Run-Hare, where shall we feed tonight? I'm starving!

The larger hare carried on cleaning her paws. *Hmm?*

Where shall we feed? Tonight? What shall we eat? He nibbled hungrily at the green beneath his feet.

You feed where you want, little broth-hare. I'm not hungry yet. I'm not done thinking.

Little-Hare thumped his foot. He was not a little leveret any more. Why did his sist-hare treat him as if he was still a newborn, when this was already his second springtime? It made him so cross. He was no younger than she, they were from the same litter. And he was just as good at racing and feeding as her, small as he was.

An all-too-familiar worry made him wince. *What are you thinking about?* he said.

Oh, nothing.

He hated it when she blocked him like this. Ever since they had lost Fath-hare and Moth-hare last summer, she had taken control, and it was so unfair. But worse, he couldn't shake the feeling, even after the many moons that had passed since, even though no one ever said anything, that somehow what had happened that terrible evening in the Wheat Between the Woods had been his fault.

The sadness was so intense he swept the feeling in the air away with his paw. *If you're not thinking about anything, why won't you come with me now? Look at all those dandelions. The wheat is showing through the

earth. We could even dare to run round the farm and see what they have spilled and left for us this time . . .*

The very last of the sun flashed in his sist-hare's eyes. *Do stop talking, little broth-hare! I am trying to concentrate. It was something one of the swallows told me, that's all. We need to prepare ourselves.*

For what? You always keep secrets from me, Run-Hare!

And you are always very nosy, little broth-hare! She turned and leapt on him, batting him with her paws, till he cried for mercy.

Get off! He slunk out from her grip, dusting himself down. He had fought back. There was strength in his legs and forefeet and claws. Of course she had won. She always did, yet he was discovering his own strength too. *Not so little any more!*

Still a bit small for your age, she said, but not unkindly.

Well, well, said a voice behind them. *If it isn't Little and Large.*

The siblings sprung around, instantly on their guard. A jack-hare. He had two extra-large front teeth, which ground together constantly, as if they had a life of their own. The sun had sunk below the hill now and was only a distant blur of foxy orange on the horizon, fringing the newcomer's fur. But it was still possible to see his scars from fight after fight.

Little-Hare watched as Run-Hare drew herself up. *Evening, Bite-Hare.*

Bite-Hare gave a short bow of his head and strutted towards them. *Evening, good look-hare. I wondered if I might have the pleasure?*

Really? sighed Run-Hare. *Coming back for more, so soon?*

Bite-Hare split his top lip, to reveal in full the oversized, grinding teeth which gave him his name. It had the effect of a human smile in a hare's face.

Call me a glutton for punishment, you beautiful creature, he said, and stood up on his hind legs, ears pricked, his paws preparing to box.

Get lost! hissed Little-Hare. *She's not in to you, isn't it obvious?*

Yes, get lost, said Run-Hare. *Go and find another jill-hare to bother. There's plenty of us around.*

I know. But you're the one I want, said Bite-Hare, and he leapt at her.

He pounced at thin air, his paws sprawling on the ground. Run-Hare was already off down the hill, dancing between the dandelions. Bite-Hare picked himself up and pounded after her with his see-saw stride.

Little-Hare sighed, and loped after them, keeping a safe distance. Further down, just as it looked as if Bite-Hare might be gaining on Run-Hare, she executed a flawless turn, and sprung to her feet, as upright as a human.

She raised her paws, preparing for combat. Skidding to a halt behind her, Bite-Hare assumed the same pose, and the two began to box.

Little-Hare didn't want to watch. It had been like this since spring arrived. Strong and clever as she was, his sist-hare was popular with many of the other jack-hares on Dandelion Hill. Bite-Hare was the most persistent. Yet no matter how powerful or good-looking these jack-hares were, how sharp they were with their paws, teeth and claws, the result of these matches with Run-Hare was always the same.

They got thrashed.

My dear, may I say you are looking absolutely ravishing tonight? oozed Bite-Hare, as he warily circled the object of his affections. *Your eyes are as bright as drops of dew on a barley head.*

Oh, really? said Run-Hare. *Well, your eyes remind me of one thing only.*

Pray, my beloved, do tell, what is that?

A target, she said, and punched him square in the face.

Little-Hare was wondering whether there might be a more romantic way to find a mate, when he felt something unexpected land on his nose.

He licked it.

At first he thought it might be blossom. But it wasn't.

Then he looked around. It was landing everywhere. On the green, the tall-homes and hedgerows, and on the squabbling hares, who paused to stare at the night sky in confusion. What had begun as a gentle trickle of flakes soon became a thick flurry.

Oblivious, Bite-Hare rubbed his bruised snout gingerly with a paw. *It doesn't matter, beautiful,* he muttered to Run-Hare, and then bared his grinding teeth. *I will do anything for your love. *Anything.**

Little-Hare frowned at the sky. *Sist-hare? Are these falling flakes what the swallows warned you about?*

No wonder she hadn't wanted to tell him.

The world was turning stranger and stranger. Last summer had been as hot as the sun itself. And yet, now – it may have been spring, but here it was, unmistakeable and very, very cold –

White. *Freezing* white.

Bite-Hare and Run-Hare were caught mid-box, their paws raised, when they felt the flakes land on their noses.

Shelter! said Run-Hare, standing down. *Everyone to the Bristly Hedge. Now!*

Hares may have been the fastest animals in the valley, but even they could not outrun the downfall, which in minutes had covered their world in layer upon layer of freezing white. They bolted across the open to a high wall of a hedge – the tallest and thickest in Old Farm – and darted under the thorns.

Bristly Hedge.

Darkness had fallen all around. From this tangly cover, they watched the white pile high around them. It was hard to believe it was still the same evening which had begun with dandelions shining and lambs playing.

Impossible. This isn't the white time of year! exploded Bite-Hare. *What will we eat? What if we freeze? What will we do?*

We will do what hares always do, said Run-Hare.

Wait, watch, and survive.

*Whatever you wish, beautiful. As long as *you* survive, that's what matters.*

Little-Hare was silent, his eyes wide in wonder. The white was mysterious and frightening, freezing over all their food – but he also wanted to run and jump and play in the big drifts. Was that so bad?

Out in the open, the dandelions were fast frozen over, the new green shoots of wheat collapsed, and the ash tall-homes creaked with their extra load. The sheep, stuck out in the open, huddled under an old and bent dead oak, as some shelter was better than none. A fox skulked by a beech on the edge of the wood, tail whisking, tasting the falling flakes suspiciously with his dark tongue. In fact, the only creature who seemed happy was the robin singing from his holly bush.

Lovely! Come on, you useless lot, this will see what you're made of! Last one in's a mayfly! Off we go!

Little-Hare watched and tried not to laugh as the bird glided out between the leaves and landed head-first in the white, his tail feathers sticking out. No one could hear what he said, but it sounded like a very muffled, *Lovely! Told you!*

The ice frosted the tawny fur of the hares and a bitter wind ruffled their whiskers. The night grew colder and longer. And a fierce hunger began to jab at their lean bellies.

*Oh, most wise and gorgeous Run-Hare, I don't think

I can stay here chewing hawthorn twigs all night long,* grumbled Bite-Hare, his mouth full of several.

'Well, if this is your idea of showing a jill-hare a good time,* said Run-Hare, *I'd hate to see a bad one.*

You mock me, beautiful, said Bite-Hare, *but one day I will convince you of my love.*

*I'm sure you will, and won't that be nice for everyone? Right. I'm the biggest and I think we should stay here under Bristly Hedge until the white has stopped falling, and then go foraging for food, if we can find any *

Can't we go out and play now? complained Little Hare. *This is so boring.*

It will be even more boring if you catch a cold and develop a fever. Run-Hare sighed. *If you think I'm going to play Moth-hare and clean the dirty white off your paws, and warm you up, you have another thing coming! We wait here until the white stops.*

But Little-Hare didn't want to wait. He thumped his paw. He was bored and hungry. Most importantly, he was fed up with being told what to do all the time. He was tired of being punished for last summer.

You know something, Run-Hare? he said. *You're right. You're not my moth-hare. You can't tell me what to do.*

And he slunk out from under Bristly Hedge, into the great white open.

What are you doing? shouted Run-Hare. *You'll catch your death!*

Bite-Hare clapped his paws together and chuckled. *Let him go! Alone at last, my love.*

But their words were lost to the wind whipping about her broth-hare's ears. The storm was much sharper and fiercer than it had looked from under the hedge. He turned around to see if his sist-hare was coming after him, but there were just swirls of white in the night, flung one way and then another, until the hedge itself was lost from view.

Better keep going, then, said Little-Hare to himself, and was surprised how small his voice sounded without anyone to hear it.

He ran on, even though the wind buffeted his face and the white chilled his paws. It was getting so deep now; it was harder to find food than he had imagined.

Hey! Perhaps there are dandelions over here, he said to himself, and dug, only there weren't. *Or maybe here!* he said, and bounded over to another spot, where there weren't any either. The more he looked and criss-crossed his own tracks, the hungrier, colder and more tired he became.

The farm dwellings, shadowy and huge, seemed to have moved, or faded into the distance. That was good, because he didn't want to run into any humans. Sometimes, on dark nights, they could be found out here, hunting with blinding lights and firesticks – and dogs.

What was less good was that that he couldn't see where he was any more, only thick sweeps of blizzard. He was so covered in white, he could have been a ghost, flitting over the open.

He grew so hungry he imagined food lying on the fresh fall. Was that paw print in fact rounds of apple peel? Were those surface scratches mouth-watering scrapings of carrot? Could those knobbly bumps be luscious kale tops? As he plunged his head and paws one last time into the white, only coming up with a few straggling, frozen stalks of thistle, he realised – he was lost.

He staggered with tiredness, wishing he had listened to Run-Hare and never left the safety of Bristly Hedge, when suddenly, he spied a miracle.

It seemed impossible, but all hares knew that miracles do happen. (For they were creatures of the moon, and what was more miraculous than that ever-transforming light in the sky?)

This miracle was smaller, but no less powerful.

Clover!

Gleaming in the light of the Swallow Moon, little dots of delicious purple-pink flowers that made his mouth salivate and his hare-hairs stand on end with excitement. Somehow it was sticking through. Delicious! His tongue was near hanging down by his claws by the time he reached it. Little-Hare opened his mouth and munched.

The clover sneezed.

Little-Hare jumped nearly as high as the stars in the sky. Before he could recover, the clover shook itself out of the white into a pink snout, followed by two surprised eyes, and a furry mound of a back. The back lurched into the air, showering the hare with powdery crumbs.

Then it was Little-Hare's turn to sneeze, shaking his whiskers. When he opened his eyes again, he could see two eyes staring at him over the damp snout.

A calf, a heifer. Only this was unlike any calf he had ever seen before. She was not nut-brown, or black and white, or even cream coloured. This calf was silvery all over. A beast that seemed to glow in the dark, as if she was carved out of ice. Yet she was most definitely alive. Now that really is a miracle, he thought joyfully.

A large tongue came out and licked him, cleaning off all the frozen white. Then the calf blinked, spotting something behind Little-Hare. She staggered straight over him, into the wind. He sprang after her as she lurched through the drifts.

But all the excitement and happiness drained away as he saw what the calf was wobbling after.

A large, motionless mound dusted with white.

Another beast, except –

He hung his head.

The body still lay where it must have fallen, the smooth ground beneath her stained deep red.

In vain, the newborn calf licked and nudged her

mother, willing for her to move, for some life to return. But Little-Hare knew that no amount of licking and nudging would ever make that chest rise and fall again, or make light return to the big, sad eyes that stared dully into space, straight through him.

He had been alone in the cold before, as hares often are, but he realised no creature was as completely alone right now as this shivering, beautiful new calf in the middle of this frozen waste.

At last the blizzard had slowed to just a few flakes drifting on the breeze. The newborn collapsed by her mother, keeping close, only the odd snuffling noise showing that she was still alive. Swollen clouds parted in the sky, allowing the full moon, the most sacred light for all creatures, to shine down on to the strange silvery calf.

As Little-Hare watched the calf's bright eyes in the dark, with so much sorrow in her cries, he suddenly knew what to say. He knew what her name should be. What her name *had* to be.

Hello, Mooncalf, he whispered. *That's the name for you. Mooncalf, as frost coloured as the white you were born on, as bright as the moonshine I see you by.* He glanced up at the sky. *Look. I'm lost too. I have no idea where we are. But from now on I promise to call this open Miracle Moor, in your honour.*

When she heard this, Mooncalf stopped her snuffling and wailing. She didn't say a word. He hopped over to her, so he was close to her soft downy head. The closer

he got, the more of a dilemma
he was in.

*Look – animals are meant to look after
their own kind, not each other. That's our
tradition, you see.*

The calf just blinked at him. She had no mother to
give her milk. He knew how it felt to lose a mother.
Silent as she may have been, Mooncalf was one of the
most precious, unusual, beautiful and wonderful creatures
he had ever seen. It might have been love, it might have
been instinct, it might have been wonder. He just *knew*.

In his short life, Little-Hare had already lost two
animals he loved. He would not lose another. He had to
do something.

In that moment, he reached out a paw to touch her
nose, and his world was changed for ever.

I will look after you, Mooncalf, he said, his teeth
chattering in his head.

In reply, she gave him another large lick with her
tongue, all over this time. Then there wasn't time for
anything more, because the hare and the calf were caught
in the glare of lights from a smoke-belching machine.

And suddenly the moonlit night was full of what
scared Little-Hare the most. More than white falling
out of winter, more than cold, more than getting lost
far from home.

Humans! Lots of them, spilling from the back of their machine.

There was the farmer; Little-Hare knew his walk even under the extra skins he was wrapped in. The farmer's mate, some workers, and a human he didn't recognise.

The stranger gave him a funny feeling. His brain pricked, sensing something he had never felt before. He should have fled already, but that pricking held him, frozen as if by a spell. Then the enchantment was broken by one of the workers, swinging their light and pointing at him, shouting –

So Little-Hare ran once more. This time, for his life.

Sit still, you scatt-harebrains! said Run-Hare. *How can we listen if you won't sit still?*

But I can't! Little-Hare had too much to get out. A hare could sit stiller than stone itself, if they wished, a skill practised from birth as a tiny leveret, frozen with terror in the long grass as a dog sniffed nearby or a falcon cried overhead. He couldn't now, though. Not after what he'd seen.

It was still dark, but Little-Hare had tracked the other two hares over the white from Miracle Moor back to the edge of Ash Wood, guided by traces of scent that they had left on hedgerow, fence post and rock.

Do what your elders and betters command! snapped Bite-Hare. He turned to Run-Hare, his mouth twisted into a leering grin. *My beauty. My love of all time. It's been such a long night. Why don't you go and dig yourself a nice warm form under the white, and I'll . . . *take care* of your foolish younger sibling?*

Little-Hare was on edge. Bite-Hare was no match for his sist-hare, but he was bigger and stronger than him. The suitor's claws were sharp, and close up, his snout was criss-crossed with scratches and scars. *Please, sist-hare. Don't leave me with him.*

Thank you for the concern, Bite-Hare, said Run-Hare, *but this concerns our litter only, and I don't need you sticking your fat paw in.* She put her nose to her broth-hare's and spoke softly. *Take a deep breath. Slow down Tell me everything. Start from the beginning.*

And he did. He told them all about getting lost in the white, mistaking Mooncalf's nose for clover, and finding her poor mother, who had lost her life bringing her calf into the world. He tried to explain how he thought that the calf was different somehow, and special, but the older hares dismissed the idea.

You did the best you could, said Run-Hare.

You silly scatt-harebrains! Your beautiful sist-hare is right, as always, Bite-Hare spat. *When are you going to learn that a hare looks after himself first? Trying to care for other creatures is not our way.*

Little-Hare knew they would never understand. They hadn't been there, out on Miracle Moor under the moon. They hadn't seen how the calf's skin shone and sparkled in the light.

So he went straight on to what happened after: the farmer and his friends, wrapped up in their wool skins, who had jumped out of their steaming vehicle, wading through the drifts towards them. He was about to tell all about the man whose very presence gave him a funny feeling, but then decided he would only get told off again, so didn't.

He told how he had watched, peeping from behind a safely distant tall-home, as they rubbed straw into Mooncalf's nose, stuck a metal stick up her rear, and smeared what looked like brown mud all over her belly. Only it hadn't smelled of mud to him, it had smelled of human magic.

Magic practised by the man whose very presence sent him strange. He twitched his nose. Just the memory made him feel peculiar.

Were they grooming her? asked Run-Hare.

Little-Hare shook his head. *I don't know. I just hope it was to make her better, not worse. Then they loaded her and the mother on to their machine and bounced all the way back to the farm.*

You shouldn't have been out there on your own! said Bite-Hare, drawing himself up, grinding his teeth. *What if you'd led the humans back to us?*

Now, now, said Run-Hare, giving Bite-Hare a light push, so that he toppled over into a soft pile of white. *Let's not get carried away, shall we? First things first. We need to go and report this news to our Wildness.*

Both the other hares recoiled in horror.

Are you mad? snarled Bite-Hare. *I mean, er, my most beautiful and radiant one, is that . . . the wisest cause of action?*

Do we have to? said Little-Hare.

No, I'm not mad, thank you, Bite-Hare, and, yes, broth-hare, we do, said Run-Hare, dusting her paws together. *Rules of this wild. All unexpected night-time deaths need to be reported by sunrise. Come on, before it's too light. We'll creep down alongside Bristly Hedge. We need to tell him the bad news ourselves, or we will be in even worse trouble if we don't.*

The hares were no stranger to Old Farm. Sometimes, when the weather was hard, a keen-eyed human might have spotted one of them nibbling at a pile of spilled grain, but they tried to stay away from this frightening home for humans, machinery and . . . dogs.

It was those four-legged friends of humans they feared the most.

The farm dogs.

There were three. Dog, the leader of the pack. It was unclear what breed he was – some form of terrier – and it was plain to all what he had been bred for. He might have been small, but what there was of him seemed all muscle and teeth. A neck as thick as a small log, and a chest broad enough to repel most counter-attacks, his face was more scarred and scraped than the entrance to a fox den.

Just the thought of him made Little-Hare feel sick to his guts.

Not to mention his two dog followers: a retired hunting hound who could still howl the valley down, and a lurcher, whose twitching gaze and spindly legs belied her incredible speed.

Worse, Dog and his followers were meant to be the Guardians of this wild. In theory, they kept the peace and protected all the beasts from unwanted intruders, animal or human. Though when they protected newborn lambs from the foxes or growing crops from the hares . . . the animals of the woods and opens had to question whose side the dogs were really on.

Not many animals could outrun a hare. But when humans picked up their firesticks, and this pack ran with them – now that was a different matter. Little-Hare shuddered, and shook the image from his mind.

Always look forward, never back! he told himself as sternly as he could, repeating one of the hare sayings he'd learned from birth.

If the farm looked scary from the ridge of Dandelion Hill, it was ten times worse close up, especially at night. Gigantic human-made beast dwellings formed canyons of iron, arranged in an impenetrable maze for any animals who didn't know their way around. Now iced

with mud-mingled white, the
yard itself was a rutted mess of machine
tracks, straw and grain, all choked up together.

I don't like it here, muttered Little-Hare.
Run-Hare shushed him, and, keeping to the darkest
shadows, they sneaked into the yard, squeezing through
a special hole in the farm's metal hedge that they had
long ago chewed open with their teeth.

Ooh, those stingers look tasty, said Bite-Hare, his teeth
chomping with excitement, as they slipped past a shock
of nettles sticking out of a pile of empty plastic sacks.

Pay attention, both of you! snapped Run-Hare. The
scents of danger were so strong that she felt sick and found
it hard to breathe. She had seen enough of what dogs
could do to last her a lifetime.

As the hares leaped over cattle grids, and ducked
down concrete alleys between the barns, Little-Hare asked the others, *Why *does* our Wildness live in such a
dangerous place?*

*If you keep asking stupid questions we might leave
you there with him,* snapped Bite-Hare.

Little-Hare scowled. It wasn't a dumb question. For
though their Wildness was the most powerful farm beast
there was, the farmer feared his power, and so had built
him a trap, which the hares now approached.

In trepidation, they crept near, ears pinned back, as they fell under its squat black shade.

Four walls of solid human stone, the kind that started as a kind of liquid wet mud, but which once dried, no claws or teeth could penetrate. It was said that the walls continued so far deep underground, even moles and worms could not find a way past. There were openings in the walls, but these were crossed with solid iron bars.

Although, as Little-Hare stood awestruck in front of the dwelling, he noticed something in the walls.

Are those cracks, sist-hare? he whispered. *Do you think it's safe? If the walls are weak he could break them down!*

Bite-Hare shushed him again, but it wasn't fair. There *was* a spreading network of spider-web thin lines, in every wall. They even seemed to tilt a little, as if the ground they stood on was unsteady. Little-Hare hoped the trap could still contain its only prisoner. First the hill, now this dwelling. Everything on Dandelion Hill was ageing and he didn't like it.

You're quite safe, broth-hare, Run-Hare replied patiently. *Even if the walls did give way, there is a heavy chain that yokes him to the ground.*

At first, the three hares could only see more early morning darkness through the bars of this trap; an empty block of shadow beyond.

Then – there was a sudden blast of steam from the shadows.

Two monstrous eyes glared in the dark.

And a huge bulk broke free from the gloom, pawing the straw-covered floor, and with a rush, flung itself at the bars with such strength and rage that the hares nearly fled straight back to Ash Wood without another word.

Run-Hare stood in front of the others, trembling before this mighty creature.

The bulging eyes considered her. Hot air curled up from the heavy nostrils, and there was a loud snort.

What creature dares disturb my rest? growled the Wildness of Old Farm.

Nearly eight feet tall, a massive two tonnes of meat and muscle, father to over two hundred calves, fed on green and human magic to be the biggest and strongest of his kind ever known, growing bigger and stronger every day.

Bull.

Run-Hare pulled Little-Hare forward, yanking him by the scruff of his neck in her jaws, just like their moth-hare used to do.

Well, go on! Tell his Wildness what you saw.

Little-Hare shivered with nerves. *Oh, Great Bull . . .*

A hoof struck the ground just behind the wall, and the tremor echoed into his guts. You could mess with some animals; all crafty hares knew that. But you never, ever, messed with a bull.

What? said Bull, who rarely used more words than he needed to. His voice was as deep and rich as the freshest furrow in a newly ploughed open.

I came to tell you . . . I mean . . .

*Find your voice, hare! Or I will find *you* when I am next free. You will pay for disturbing me.*

I'm sorry, Little-Hare said, looking down at the slushy ground, as the very first light of pre-dawn glimmered in the sky. He didn't know how to speak to this mighty being.

You will be if you don't find your voice!

Come on, broth-hare! hissed Run-Hare.

Little-Hare struggled. Sorrow twisted around his throat like a snare. What he had seen under the moonlight was more than simply the death of one animal, and the birth of another. It was the beginning of something. He just didn't know what.

You know the heifer, who was carrying your calf— he started.

What of her? Has she borne yet?

She has, but . . . Little-Hare was learning to choose his words carefully, as his kind always did.

*Curse you hares, and your caution and cunning! Speak plainly, or I will break these bars, and I will break *you.**

I'm sorry. Something went wrong. There was too much frost. I couldn't do anything . . . she didn't survive.

At first there was silence. The hares glanced at one another. Then there was a deep sigh, another cloud of steam snorting into the air, a paw of the ground. Little-Hare trembled some more, as the bull bellowed.

It was no ordinary bellow, but one so long, loud and full of sorrow, that the hares' ears flinched with pain at the sound. The bellow sailed out past the bars of the bull's pen, and through the stone holes of the farm. It squeezed between bales of hay wrapped tight in plastic, rippled the puddles in the slushy ground, and rattled the windows of the old farmhouse.

A bellow that every living creature for miles around must have heard:

> *Then! Let the waters cover the earth once more.*
> *Let the sun turn the sky bright with flame*
> *Let the ice cover the land which is left*
> *And so ends our dream, as it began.*
> *In darkness and in silence.*
> *The silence of the end.**

They were lines from an animal dream, their version of myths, passed down from generation to generation. This verse was from the oldest animal dream of all, that told of how all creatures came into the world . . . but also how they would one day leave it.

Out in the white-covered open, the sheep and lambs looked up from the tufts they gnawed at through the cold. The chickens in their metal dwelling stopped pecking at grain, and the goats butted the planks of their pens in response. All the cows raised their heads from their troughs of feed, and even the dreaded dogs howled at the end of their chains. The wrens cried in the hedgerows, the rooks screeched in their nests, and the foxes barked in the woods.

Every creature of the valley heard the mourning of their bull.

As this wave of sadness broke over their heads, the hares looked around them, ears twitching with worry.

Oh, perfect! Now every human on the farm will be wide awake, said Bite-Hare. *We should go. Now!*

The other two ignored him, lost in the gaze of their Wildness, his call of grief. Bull pressed his head right against the bars, his breath steaming over Little-Hare. Hotter than blood it felt to him, the giant eyes straining as if they might pop clean free of his skull. But the mighty creature's voice was now little more than a whisper.

And this calf . . . what of it?

She is alive, Great Bull, but—

Describe her to me! Quick! We do not have long.

In the near distance, there was the sound of doors opening, the cries of men and women. Human lights lit up the grey dawn. The three dogs no longer howled, but barked and barked, a living alarm. Little-Hare looked at Run-Hare, unsure whether to carry on, but she prodded him forward, her eyes softening.

Go on, she said with kindness. *We will be fast enough when we need to be.*

The strangest calf I ever saw, Bull. A shining silver-white all over, the same colour as the moonlight by which she showed herself to me, which was how I chose her name.

Mooncalf! said Bull. He strained at the chain holding him to the wall so hard that crumbs of concrete rattled down from around the solid iron ring that fixed it there. *Please tell me you did not call her that!*

43

How did you know? trembled Little-Hare. *Was that . . . bad?*

Bad? It was foretold, you idiot!

The human voices were closer now. Little-Hare was tired and cold. The day was about to begin, they were in dangerous territory, and the enemy was approaching. Behind him, Bite-Hare fretted to Run-Hare.

My gorgeous jill-hare . . . we should run! Now! Come on!

He turned to flee, but Run-Hare stayed him with a paw.

I don't know where Mooncalf is, said Little-Hare to the bull. *The humans have taken her somewhere on the farm, to do their magic. It will have to be extra-strong magic. She had been out in the cold for so long, without warmth, without milk . . .*

Bull threw himself against the wall again. The hares glanced at one another, wondering how many times he needed to do so before it split in two.

Fool-hare to let her out of your sight! Mooncalf is no ordinary newborn; she is the last of her kind.

How were we meant to know, your Wildness? said Run-Hare. *You know that humans take all animals from us as they please, especially calves. Many bulls are slaughtered young, and the heifers make milk for them for the rest of their lives. Great Bull, explain yourself.*

The mooncalf must be saved. She will never make milk or become meat, but she must be saved! Their great leader sounded so vulnerable. *Do you understand, hares? That

44

dream I sang tells of the end of our world. But do you not know how the end of the world begins?*

Little-Hare scratched his head. *I'm sure Moth-hare did tell me; I'm trying to remember.*

Bull sighed. *Did you pay *any* attention when your moth-hare and fath-hare taught you the laws of the wild?*

Sure! said Little-Hare, sticking his chest out. *When an animal dies, the sky weeps tears.* He looked up at the few flakes still gently falling. *Sometimes very cold white ones. And when the last animal in the world dies, there will be the storm of storms. Oh, and *never* try and steal a fresh dandelion out of my sist-hare's mouth, because—*

Silence! Do you remember the verses of the animal dream, which describe the events that will lead to the end of all things? Perhaps you all need reminding? The verse tells of a calf the colour of moonlight, her mother lost, discovered by a little one.

I'm in the dream of all animals? Little-Hare's eyes widened.

A little one that must save the mooncalf to avoid what follows. For if you do not save her by midsummer, the night of the full Cow Moon, there will be a great Terribleness.

I know that verse backwards! said Bite-Hare. *It could be about anything! It says little one, not little hare, and that is not the first moon-white calf born on this farm, she can't be!*

There are other omens too, said the bull. *White out

of winter, a great wet destroying the land, burning fires . . . these are all warnings of a Terribleness.*

You see! gloated Bite-Hare. *None of that has happened. The white falling could just be a coincidence.*

But if it is true, said Run-Hare, *how can we stop it?*

According to the dream, only Little-Hare can! thundered the bull. *You must save Mooncalf to stop the Terribleness. Or we all perish.*

Little-Hare's heart felt as if it wanted to leap out of his chest and run over the hills and far away. Mooncalf had already been taken by the humans on their machine.

How? he whimpered. *I am just a little hare. How can I save a mooncalf?*

You must! You are chosen! They heard the unmistakable sound of booted feet thumping down the track towards them, accompanied by the worst sound a hare can hear.

The galumphing paws and hot panting breath of—

Dogs! screamed Bite-Hare, and like that, all three were off, running faster than fear itself.

Stranger still, even as Little-Hare ran, hurtling for his life, there was that feeling again. The feeling he had in the white on Miracle Moor, from the new human on the farm. His ears and brain prickled with oddness, until he heard the bull roaring after them.

It will be the end of us, beasts and humans alike. Do you hear?

Little-Hare did hear, but the bull's final words were

distant echoes as all the hares hurtled away from the humans and their slavering dogs, bounding up the hill, as the chilly dawn finally broke over the valley.

Their first priority was to find comfort and warmth, to dig their hidden lairs in the white, and rest. But Little-Hare found no comfort or warmth in their leader's final words, which reverberated in his ears like the ancient howls of mysterious time itself, forever at his heels with unforgiving and all-consuming jaws.

Save the mooncalf and stop the Terribleness or face the end of everything. The end of the world!

Little-Hare could not sleep.

He had clambered into his frosty shallow form, dug out of the white between two ridges at the top of the hill, and squatted, pressing his downy body close to the earth. Resting his nose on his forefeet, he glared briefly at the white-swept hill and made sure his head was set against the wind, in case any unwelcome visitors were prowling the wastes beyond, searching for scent.

Then, eyes glassed over, he waited.

He waited and waited. He shivered and writhed, waiting for drowsiness to fall behind his eyes, but it never did. There was little to do in a hare's form but dream, and he couldn't even manage that.

For instead there was a voice inside his head that would not let him go. Bull's bellow, his warning of a Terribleness coming. What even was this Terribleness and how could he, a little hare, stop it? How would saving Mooncalf stop such a thing, and who or what was he saving her from?

You are chosen!

He started upright, as the bull's words echoed again in his mind, scattering the white that covered him. His nose inhaled the scents of morning, his amber eyes adjusting to the bright dawn. The small breathing holes either side of him among the stalks poking through the white suggested that Run-Hare and Bite-Hare still slumbered on.

So he did not move at first, but instead, did what hares do best.

He listened.

He swivelled his long black-tipped ears, together. They scooped the sounds of spring into his chiselled head.

The many birds of the forest were still loud and strong, welcoming the new morning in.

The robin sang his cheery tune from inside his holly bush, as he did every day.

*If anyone comes near me, I am absolutely going to deck them. Is that crystal clear? The lot of you! This is *my* bush, so back off!*

Little-Hare was not sure why anyone else would want the robin's holly bush, so he turned his ears some more, and caught the rooks, gossiping to one another as they flapped their glossy, ragged wings down from their overstuffed nests to hunt for the early worm.

What do you reckon to Bull's dream, what do you reckon, what do you reckon?

Load of old bull, mate, so to speak, so to speak!

He said the end of the world was coming! A Terribleness, he called it, he called it!

It'll be the end of your world in a minute, in a minute, in a minute, if you don't stop yakking and watch where you're going—

There was a sudden caw of surprise, as one of the speakers crashed into a tall-home.

Told you! Now are you going to help yank out these worms or what?

All the voices of Dandelion Hill were joined together, from bright-voiced blackbirds to warbling skylarks, cheerful and unbowed by the bull's solemn warning, his bellows heard across the whole valley. Little-Hare felt his muscles unknot. The previous night seemed a lifetime away. The white would melt, flowers would eventually recover from the sudden shock, and the world would carry on, just as it always had. Mooncalf would be looked after. The humans knew what they were doing.

Animals called their stories dreams, and perhaps that's all this one truly was, a made-up story to scare young hares. Or worse, a nightmare, to keep him awake during the day.

You're going mad, Little-Hare said to himself. *The world isn't going to end! Not today, at least.*

50

Everything was going to be fine. He rubbed his face clean, licked his paws, and wiped his precious ears. But just as he was doing this, they tuned into another voice, an unfamiliar one, saying strange words in a stranger tongue. The speaker suddenly swooped down in front of him.

It was a waxwing, a regular seasonal visitor to the valley.

She was small, with a very distinctive pale reddish crest, and a black mask around the eyes. These dark eyes burned deep into the hare's soul, as she flapped her yellow and white wings.

The bird's crested top and bright markings struck him as a flame in the morning haze, and her solemn voice lent every word the quality of prophecy.

Little-Hare! I am a young bird, announced the waxwing. *I have come from the northern countries of forests, lakes and ice. I have been here since winter, feasting on your delicious berries. I should have gone back already, but NO! I CAN'T! Do you know why?*

The hare shook his head.

I am still here to tell you that the world is in TROUBLE.

Seriously? Not again! said Little-Hare. He wasn't sure he could take much more bad news.

Yes, again! Look around you! It should not be white on the ground now. It was too hot last summer. The weather is changing. You think everything is fine in this green valley of yours, but I cannot leave it without telling you that the rest of the world is on FIRE! Humans are flooding to this island because it is the only place left they can live! I have flown over the world's sea to get here, and it is rising, unstoppably! You think your bull is lying? That a Terribleness could not happen here? THINK AGAIN!

The waxwing paused briefly to preen her magnificent feathers. Then she was off again. *Food is already in short supply! I nearly didn't fly, to save energy, even though I come here every winter, without fail.*

How else would you have got here?

I would have walked! Does it matter? I am here. And I am telling you that you must take the warning of Bull seriously. We all heard him in the valley last night, they probably heard him in the next valley along too, he was so loud! You are chosen to stop this Terribleness. If you don't save the mooncalf, there will be much worse things to follow. Why does it take a young bird from a faraway land to point this out to you?

What kind of worse things?

A great wet covering the earth, drought, burning fires – there are too many to count! What are YOU going to do about them? The bird shook her head, her pale crest quivering with impatience.

Little-Hare tried to choose his words carefully. *I'm waiting for my sist-hare to wake up, and Bite-Hare . . . then I was going to talk to them, and I might see if some of the other animals could help us save Mooncalf, perhaps . . . maybe that kind of thing?*

Waxwing half flew off the ground in fury.

Going to . . . Might . . . What are you going to do about it NOW, hare?

Right now?

No, tomorrow, or maybe in a year's time, when the mooncalf is gone and the Terribleness has ended the world, and we are all dead. Did you not hear Bull about the other omens? A great wet! Fires! Of course RIGHT NOW!

The hare thought very hard and gave the answer he imagined she wanted to hear, that might make her leave him in peace. *Should I . . . find out where Mooncalf is?*

Waxwing dropped back to the ground with a sigh. *Finally!* She groomed her feathers as if they had personally insulted her. Then she looked up again. *Why am I even still talking to you? You are chosen! WHY ARE YOU STILL HERE LOOKING AT ME?*

Little-Hare began to run.

He didn't just run to find Mooncalf, of course. He ran to get away.

Why can't you all leave me alone? he cried out to the empty hillside, and to the voices in his head – the bull bellowing about the end of the world, Waxwing urging him to hurry up and the other two hares telling him what to do all the time.

Most of all, he ran from the sorrow he could not shake in his heart, stirred up again by the bull's grief for his mate. Last summer. Out of nowhere, his moth-hare and fath-hare, bolting through the wheat towards him, screaming something he didn't understand –

Until it was too late.

His moth-hare's face stretched tight in terror. Fath-hare's cries of pain.

Little-Hare had been there. He could have helped them. But he didn't.

He wanted to run and run, run so fast until time itself reversed, and could be lived afresh.

Don't care, he told himself, trying to feel braver. *Have to get away!*

The noise in his head grew fainter and fainter, like a distant echo, the more he ran. It was still cold, and the air felt bitter against his eyes as it flew past. His paws were a furry blur over the white. As he raced down the slope from Ash Wood to the farm, he sniffed, looked and listened, alert to even the smallest sound of danger. Away from the frosted hedge, he ran in plain sight, leaving neat little tracks behind him.

Below, lights were already on in the farmhouse, smoke curling, their machines growling with life. The dogs barked and barked, and a crow cawed somewhere, shattering the wintery calm.

Voices, promises and commands jumped all over the hare's brain like hay seeds caught in a gust of wind. White – against which their earth-coloured camouflage was no use – was no friend to brown hares.

*Might as well be leaving drops of blood saying *food over here*,* Little-Hare muttered to himself as he sprinted.

He was following a hare-way, known only to his kind,

the fastest route to the meuse in the metal hedge. His hind legs flew so fast, they barely touched the ground, leaving the faintest of marks. Steam curled up from his maw as he scuttered down in a figure of eight.

Suddenly, the world felt quiet again. The distant snoring of badgers in their setts, hedgehogs dozing in their nests, even the birds had now fallen silent. As if they had vanished on a signal. That was never good. He paused for a moment, every muscle primed.

Then he saw it.

A large shadow soaring over the ground, sharp edged by the sun. And now Little-Hare heard it too, an unmistakeable and piercing cry; the one call he feared more than a dog's.

The cry of death to small hares.

A buzzard.

Little-Hare had to think fast. That was a hare's second weapon after his speed – his cunning. Could he outwit his enemy? He swerved off his hare-way, and the hunting bird swerved too.

It was too late to race up the hill now, and he could feel the shadow on his back. A fierce pair of wings that wanted to close over him for ever. No matter how much freezing air he sucked into his aching chest, no matter how much his legs powered and spun through the white, he couldn't shake it.

Little-Hare was alone and exposed in a wintry desert. He ran this way, then that –

Leave me alone! he cried out desperately. *I'm chosen! I'm following Bull's dream, that's all. I'm going to save Mooncalf!*

The bird gave no reply in the shared tongue, other than the shrill cry which all living creatures can hear. Little-Hare tried not to think about the hares he had seen plucked from an open by strong claws just like those about to grab him.

He was not fast enough.

With a thump, the claws clutched at his back, tearing the fur, piercing the skin. Little-Hare shrieked in terror, and the bird bounced off into the air again.

And then Little-Hare tripped over.

You're going too fast downhill again, he could hear Run-Hare saying, but she wasn't here now. This wasn't a pretend race or a mating ritual, this was life and death, tumbling over and over. His world upside down, with beating outstretched wing, a beak jabbing for his eyes –

No, please, not my eyes!

He was on his back, screaming louder than a human baby, his eyes rolling with fear, his heart pumping blood into his brains so fast he couldn't think.

A talon scraped the skin of his pale belly, drawing blood.

You can't do that! gasped Little-Hare.

The talon paused for a moment, mid-slice.

Don't take this the wrong way, said the buzzard, her eyes glowing like ripe corn, *but nothing puts me off my food more than when it starts to talk back.*

Buzzard's talons seized the hare, and she flapped her wings, lifting him off the ground. Little-Hare felt the earth fall away, his stomach lurched, and his body jerked. This was, he knew, how death could come for his kind. Sudden and sharp out of a clear, cold sky.

And at the very edge of his vision, as the buzzard hauled him up and over the open, he spied a flash of sunlight on the iron roof of the bull's dwelling.

A Terribleness was coming – if he didn't save Mooncalf in time.

For a moment, the buzzard's cruel gaze blurred into the flame-crested stare of Waxwing, whose voice echoed in his head.

I don't care that she's about to kill you! We will all die if you don't do something! When are you going to hurry up and DO SOMETHING?

Her fury passed into his veins and merged with his own, creating fire. Was this attack his punishment for running away? For failing his moth-hare and fath-hare? *Not again.* Almost as a reflex, his cunning hare-brain told him what to do. Little-Hare made himself go limp in the buzzard's grip. He felt the talons relax a little in his skin.

This is not my time, bird, he whispered.

His captor twitched.

What did you say?

I said, this is not my time!

And Little-Hare lunged up and battered the buzzard

on her belly. He kicked and punched so hard that the bird began to weave through the air. As he fought, he screamed, but this time it wasn't a scream of terror, only a cry of rage and determination.

Not his time to die, not now. He had to make amends for his failure last summer. He had to do something right, just for once.

With frenzied shrieks, the buzzard and hare ploughed into a stand of frost-capped reeds sticking out of a marshy dell at the bottom of the hill. They rolled over one another in a whirling wheel of wing and paw. Little-Hare rose to his hind legs with a glare of gleaming eyes, his top lip split, his teeth poking through. The buzzard flew and kicked at him.

Hares don't fight back! she spluttered.

This one does. What are you going to do about it?

He launched one last punch, so hard that the buzzard reeled up into the air, shedding feathers in a spray of blood, showering the pristine white around them.

You have to play by the rules! the buzzard spat. *You are my prey! The laws of nature apply to you, hare, as they do to us all.*

Little-Hare licked blood off his paw. *You heard the bull, same as the rest of us. I've been chosen to save Mooncalf. If I don't, a Terribleness will come! A great wet, fires, the end of the world – you heard him.*

So? What am I meant to live on? Air?

I'm sure you'll figure something out, muttered the hare, and loped off through the stiff reeds. He felt dizzy. Somehow, he was moving towards the farm.

We can't just change overnight, you know! yelled the buzzard, now circling safely high in the sky again. *My kind have eaten hares for thousands of moons! The weird weather has created a shortage of shrews! If I die of starvation, you'll only have yourself to blame . . .*

I'll learn to live with it, said Little-Hare to himself, as the angry screams of the bird faded away. He was injured. He needed somewhere dark and warm to lie in. Without thinking, he squeezed through his meuse in the farm's metal hedge, pushing the chewed wires apart. But as their ragged tips scraped his underside, he shrank back.

The wires were now tipped with blood from the slice the buzzard had made in his belly. His shoulders dipped as he looked back at the hill. He was too tired to run all the way up now.

Just need . . . find somewhere to rest . . . that's all, he muttered to himself.

But the moment he crossed through the fence, his nerves started jangling again. It had been bad enough visiting the bull before dawn – it was madness in daylight. The air was already thick with the stink of human . . . and much worse, Dog and his accomplices.

His ears scooped up the noise of distant machines

humming, a faint murmur of human chatter somewhere, and thankfully – dogs snoring. This would buy him moments, but not many.

Little-Hare flopped towards a shady square of the farm he knew, away from the house. If he looked down, he saw gleaming drops of black blood vanishing into ice-fragmented puddles beneath his feet. He had to ignore them for now, as he turned the corner into the yard.

Sparse spring sun fell here, in this damp spot, home only to abandoned pallets, dirty barrels, and old farm machinery, dumped to rust into oblivion.

All of which made what sat in the middle of the half-yard even more strange.

It was new.

A large, low, rectangular box, set on its own away from the piles of junk. Sleek metal walls with no holes to let in light or air that the little hare could see. Just a box, resting on four great wheels. Perhaps it had been moved here, rather than built in this lonely spot?

Cautiously, sniffing the air, Little-Hare approached. Even simple movements were an effort now. The blood would not stop. It ran hot and thick down his back legs. He would lie down and rest in a moment. Everything was going to be fine.

He sniffed the tracks and pattern of footprints in the muddy white. The box itself gave off an alien scent of human magic that made his eyes water and scalded his nostrils.

The magic he had smelled on Miracle Moor the

night before.

Mooncalf! he croaked.

His new friend was inside here, he was sure of it! Wires and pipes spooled out of one end, running into the ground, as if the box had sprouted roots. Little-Hare sniffed and sniffed around the edges, trying to find a way in.

He was so low to the ground as he explored that he didn't notice the small black orbs, perched on the corners of the cabin, that swivelled and whirred as they tracked his every move.

Little-Hare's vision swam, turning the day dark.

His head spun.

I think I need to lie down, he said to the empty yard.

He lurched towards a cluster of plastic barrels, heading for the long weeds that sprouted between them. But he never got that far.

His eyes wide open in shock, he toppled over on to the wet stone. Little-Hare stared but could not see. The blood leaking from his belly made sure of that. His body was beginning to give up.

So he did not see the notice above the door to the container. Animals could not read human signs or symbols as a rule, but he might have just understood this one. In black on bright yellow, it carried a human skull and two crossed bones.

FACTORIUM FOODS FIELD LABORATORY
MASKS AND PROTECTIVE CLOTHING
ESSENTIAL

He did not see the door suddenly swing open, either.

A masked figure in a rubber suit and boots marched out. The stranger scooped the unconscious creature up in his gloved hands and carried him back inside the sealed box, the door closing with a hiss behind them.

Outside in the yard, a flurry of fresh daytime white came down, burying the scattered drops of dark blood, the only clue that the little hare had ever been there in the first place.

When dusk arrived later that evening on Dandelion Hill, the robin roused the animal wanderers of the night with his usual call, echoing so melodically from the holly bush.

I swear on my life, if anyone looks at me, yeah, they are dead! Jog on!

The older hares stirred from their drowsy rest, shaking and brushing the white away, noticing that even more seemed to have fallen while they were asleep. Run-Hare stretched and yawned, looking around, sniffing the evening air. Bite-Hare tried to sniff her and was rebuffed with a firm paw in the ear.

The crueller you are to me, my Run-Hare, he purred, *the deep-hare my affection grows—*

Oh, do shut up, Bite-Hare! she said. *I've only just woken up and already you're boring me asleep again. If you carry on, I shall make you look after Little-Hare all night, just to punish you.*

If it would make you happy, nothing would give me greater pleasure than to take care of your younger broth-hare— He stopped, ears swivelling. *Except, I think we might need to find out where he is, first.*

Run-Hare leapt over to where Little-Hare had dug his form. The faint shallow was empty, and half-filled with fresh white. She put her nose to it, inhaling his scent, and beat the ground with her hind feet in frustration.

Why will he never do what he's told? And it's always me who has to pick up the pieces, Bite-Hare, always me.

She lolloped off towards the wood, thinking Little-Hare might have taken shelter from the second whitefall under its canopy. Halfway there, she turned around and frowned at Bite-Hare, who was now flopping along, trying to catch up with her.

*Do you have to follow me *everywhere*? I can handle this.*

Run-Hare shook her head and darted off into the wood, but this did not stop Bite-Hare.

My love! Don't leave me! I beg your forgiveness! I will do anything . . . His eyes seemed to turn quite black in the shade. *Anything.*

Little-Hare was also in a wood. He was running between the tall-homes, slower than he ever had in his life. They were stark and bare, and terror lay all around, but he knew he had to keep going, till everything awful was far behind him.

It was hard, though, because a bird was stuck to his stomach, poking and clawing at his belly, even as he dragged the creature over the roots and shallows of the walk-upon.

Everyone was shouting at him to go faster. Run-Hare, Bite-Hare, Waxwing, Bull, they were everywhere and nowhere, yelling at him. Fath-hare and Moth-hare screaming. A buzzard screeched.

This can't be right, he said to no one in the dream. *You're making a mistake. A big mistake. I'm the chosen one!*

But a blood red tidal wave of terror just surged behind him, pulling tall-homes out by their roots, seeping in between every one, drowning everything in its way, threatening to curl over him at any moment—

Little-Hare awoke with a start. *Help me!* he screamed.

There was something pulling at his belly, but it wasn't a buzzard's claw.

A tiny metal twig, weaving in and out of his skin, drawing it tight together, held by human hands cased in a smooth and stretchy second skin. He panicked, and writhed, trying to escape, but it felt like tough briars were binding him, holding him down tight. The human cursed, and then Little-Hare felt a sharp prick in his leg, and he returned to the blood-filled woods of his mind.

*

Run-Hare was frustrated, and Bite-Hare was exhausted. They had searched Ash Wood, the entire length of Bristly Hedge, and the open, but there was no sign of Little-Hare.

In the woods, the robin told them he hadn't seen the younger hare, and that if he had, he would have given him what for. The noisy rooks were no more helpful, as they returned to their messy nests after a day of foraging.

Can't you see, can't you see, we've got enough to do, feeding our young, mending our nests, without worrying about where your little one has got to! Every animal to their own! Every animal to their own!

But I think he might have done something stupid, called out Run-Hare. *Gone off on his own again. You know what he's like.*

Well, then, cawed one of the rooks. *Serve him right, serve him right!*

Run-Hare glowered at them, but Bite-Hare just nudged her with his nose.

Come on, my beautiful, he said. *Let's keep looking.*

It was dark by the time they found the blood in the reeds at the bottom of the hill. They had been running in loops, back on themselves, calling in vain, asking every animal they saw, with no luck, when they came upon the marsh.

Afterwards, they couldn't remember who had first caught the scent, whether it had been Run-Hare or Bite-Hare who had started scooping the white away. But it was definitely Run-Hare who saw the spattered spots of red across the ground, crystallised like frozen poppies, shining in the moonlight.

She fell on her paws, and howled to that same miraculous moon above that guided all hares through the dark.

It was their greatest source of wonder. This distant, shining light which appeared, and grew, then disappeared, and appeared again. For a moon never died, it only changed. Though hares could and did die, all too often, as she tried not to remember.

Poor Little-Hare still blamed himself for last summer, she knew, when it had been nothing to do with him. She stared at the magical sphere hanging in the sky, and wished for a miracle: that Little-Hare could appear right now, that she could lay a comforting paw on his back.

But there were no miracles tonight.

Bite-Hare wanted to comfort Run-Hare too. He wanted to play the big hare, the kindly one. He did, in his hare-heart, want to show true love. Perhaps even more, he wanted to be loved, which he never ever had been, not by his fath-hare or moth-hare, who had both called him ugly and big toothed. The more he dwelt on this, the more he just wanted to say something, anything, that would make Run-Hare love him.

So he said, poking around, *Some feathers here too, as well as fur . . . I suspect it was a buzzard that cruelly ripped your broth-hare from us.*

It did not make her love him. She stared at him, eyes brimming with anguish.

He's gone! My little broth-hare! And it was my fault! I should never have let him leave the hedge in the first place.

Well. Can't be helped, my love. It's nature's way . . .

Her hare features contorted into something so snarled up with rage that Bite-Hare had to retreat. Run-Hare jabbed a paw at him, claws outstretched as she spoke.

Then I have had enough of nature's way! Fath-hare! Moth-hare! And now Little-hare! Must I always lose the ones I love?

He wheedled. *You're upset, my sweetness. But you will never lose me, I promise.*

No! Run-Hare was rocking, retching. She stood on her hind legs, her paws raised as if to fight, striking a long-eared silhouette against the great silent disc in the sky. She boxed the distant globe. *I would rather be as lonely as that moon above our heads than have you.*

*

69

After the blood-red wood, Little-Hare had been swimming in the fish-road. He was pulled deep under the surface by a powerful current, down into the murky depths. But now he found himself, at last, surfacing again. His eyes opened once more.

Roots, in the form of cow-skin straps, bound him to a flat surface. A transparent worm appeared to be feeding on his rear haunch, where a neat square of his fur had been removed. But most amazing of all, his belly had healed. White material was wrapped around it tight in strips, which felt both sore and weird, but at least there was no more blood.

He still felt the drowsy depths of the fish-road and the darkness of the woods in his mind, threatening to drag him back under at any moment, but he had enough strength to gently roll his head and see where he was.

A dim indoor space, which reeked of human magic and cleanliness. Hares did not belong indoors! His frightened hare face was reflected back at him in dozens of glass bottles and jars. A constant drone of low-level humming and beeps. It was louder than a corn open in summer, though he saw no bees or birds, only alien and inanimate objects of human magic.

Little-Hare struggled against his bonds, but he was trapped tight. His eyes rolled right back into his head as a shadow fell over him.

He recognised the purple-clad hands from before, the ones which stitched him back together. The rest of the body was now visible: covered in pigeon-egg coloured shapeless material, half the face masked off, only the clear, watery eyes visible.

Overcome by fear, Little-Hare was unable to stop himself raving, even though he knew his human captor would not be able to understand him.

What is this place? Why am I here? Have you got Mooncalf too? What have you done with her? Bull told us she was in danger! He bared his teeth in frustration. *Am I going to be killed? You know I'm chosen, right? Why can't humans understand animals? I just wish you could talk to me!*

His captor's eyes softened above the mask. Was that a smile?

But that's just it . . . little one, he said. *I can.*

PART 2:
WHAT ARE
YOU GOING
TO DO?

The day after Little-Hare disappeared, the white began to melt. It slowly receded, a great sheet pulled back from the green valley, shrinking into the edges and corners, seeping into the soft ground, sliding off leaves and roofs or melting into air, until only the most stubborn patches of ice remained in the coldest and loneliest parts of Dandelion Hill. And where it had melted away, more and more cracks began to appear in the earth beneath. The ground the animals lived on was changing right under their feet.

Spring returned, slowly merging into summer. Ash Wood came into leaf, often the last in the valley to do so. Bristly Hedge became more blossom than bristle. Run-Hare and Bite-Hare waited, but as the days came and went, any hope of ever seeing Little-Hare again faded.

Life carried on around Old Farm, all the same.

Nodding cowslips shone in the warming sun, crowds of tender bluebells jostled for space across the woodland floor, and everything grew. Occasionally, a nightingale could be heard singing as the soft nights turned longer and lighter.

It was a magical song, near impossible to describe, but those who were privileged to hear it never ever forgot. Apart from, that is, a couple of dormice who made their dwelling in the same bit of scrub as the trilling bird.

What do you think? said one to her mate, as they were serenaded for yet another night.

I preferred her old stuff, to be honest, he said, scraping at a nut clamped between his paws.

But even with all this beauty and mystery, the idyllic early summer of Dandelion Hill would not have been complete without its most vital ingredient.

Visitors.

From the reed warblers in the low wetland, filling the marshy beds with their chirrupy tune, to the swifts sailing high in the deepening blue skies, the valley came alive with the rich and varied presence of so many visitors from so many different countries. They came to both partake in and enrich the life of Old Farm.

The most distinctive of them was the cuckoo, whose mysterious clocklike call usually announced the arrival of spring. The birds were late this year, again, so they announced the arrival of summer instead. No one knew what the call meant, for the word *cuckoo* in the animal tongue simply meant . . . 'cuckoo'.

It was this visitor's chiming cry that accompanied Run-Hare a whole moon later, as she at last accepted that Little-Hare was not ever coming back. They had searched for many nights. They had waited for many days. They had put the word out to other wilds.

Now another full moon was here, the time had come to accept the unthinkable.

And it was not just any full moon, but a giant disc of pale pink that bathed Run-Hare and Bite-Hare in its milky light.

A Hare Moon.

This was the most miraculous of all moons, for its rose-coloured light always heralded the rebirth of the world they knew, shining down upon clouds of blossom, flowers and green growth. A light to celebrate all the new animals about to make their way in life.

But there was little to celebrate this night. By the Hare Moon's glimmer, the pair followed the furrows of a hare-way to a desolate, marshy heath far above the gentle woods and opens of Dandelion Hill. Not much stood here, just springy coils of bracken, the odd dead tall-home and . . . a circle of ancient, oddly shaped boulders.

No one knew how so many large and similar-sized rocks had come to be in one place, arranged in one of nature's most favoured shapes, a circle. The shape of a hare eye, the shape of the sun. Had they been thrown there by a storm of storms? Or tumbled down from a mountain top that no longer existed? Perhaps even placed deliberately by some supernatural force?

It was impossible to say for sure. But the mystery of the place was one reason that drew hares from far and wide, when the Hare Moon appeared, to sit in a circle around the rocks. Few humans had ever witnessed this sacred ceremony, and those who had always misunderstood it.

Just hares feeding together, said some. It only happens to *look* like a circle, claimed others. A hare parliament, declared a few, or a council. *Witches!* said those who always thought anything happening in the countryside at night had to involve witches.

It wasn't for any of those things.

It was a ring of grief.

Run-Hare arrived well after midnight, her fur shining silver in the moonlight. Bite-Hare followed at a respectful pace behind, clutching a small wreath of ivy and blackcurrants between his jaws.

Blackcurrants? hissed one of the other jack-hares in the circle, keeping his head bowed. *During a Hare Moon? Impossible!*

But it was so hot at the end of winter, don't you remember? whispered his jill-hare. *The dandelions came early. And then the white fell. Everything's gone so strange. I don't understand it. Half the birds who normally come to the valley aren't here this year. Those cuckoos were late, again. Not to mention the cracks in the ground, the fish-roads running low. I think even some of these rocks have moved . . .*

There was no time to talk more, as the funeral party reached the ring of stones. Bite-Hare laid down the wreath, and Run-Hare nudged it with her nose, before beginning to sing. She sang a call of loss for her broth-hare. It celebrated him for being so little and brave, lost in a pledge to another beast's dream, taken from them by a bird of prey, as was nature's way.

Then, something incredible started to happen – something none of the hares had ever seen before.

For as Run-Hare sang, a light appeared in the centre of the circle. A spark, that swelled into a glow, and then expanded into a gaseous ball of fire, the colour of a wild rose, which hovered and blazed.

Was it the pale pink of the Hare Moon, reflected off a shining stone? Some might have called it a will o' the wisp or a fairy fire; others might have blamed natural gases in the marsh, or even glow worms.

Who could really say? Stranger things have happened at midnight on the moors. The hares only knew what they saw.

A wondrous light that burned and danced in the dark.

And as Run-Hare kept singing, so the ball of flame grew and spun, a funnelled tornado of phosphorescence that whirled greedily over the rough ground, as if it wished to gather up all that was light in the world.

The hare's words echoed into the night sky, circling over the heads of the mourners like a flock of crows, before dispersing into the darkness. Then came a low hum, rising to a wail of sadness, from the other hares. For now the gathering mourned not just Little-Hare, but all those they had lost.

Then, the most miraculous thing on a night of miracles.

As the watching hares peered with amazement into the twisting tower of light, spiralling into the sky above their heads, they saw not just sparks and flame, but visions.

Those they had lost.

An old fath-hare strangled in a snare. Two leverets snatched by a fox. A family of hares poisoned by a freshly sprayed open.

The earth remembered them. The moon welcomed them.

Run-Hare's ghostly chorus had conjured up, over this blasted and barren spot, a hovering, glowing carousel of all the forgotten, the hares no longer here. The gossiping jack-hares were struck dumb. Run-Hare was lost in her reverie, and even Bite-Hare could do nothing but watch, wide-eyed, as the lost hares in the fire spun faster and faster, brighter and brighter, until with a flash – all were gone.

Run-Hare stopped singing.

They had lost all sense of time and now a foxglove-tinged dawn rose around them, every watching hare stunned into silence. Not least because many of the mourners knew they could be next. This gathering of hares, a few of them very old and white whiskered indeed, knew it was growing harder and harder to find places to hide from human danger.

But Run-Hare was not frightened. She was not fully sure what the opposite of fear was, though whatever it was, she felt it.

A kind of readiness.

Don't you see what this means? she said to the other hares, who were still afraid. *Dreams are true. We can see them. Dreams are real.*

My love, are you sure that was a dream? said Bite-Hare. *It was certainly very mysterious, but whatever it was, I'm sure there is a perfectly sensible explanation. You are lost in grief for your broth-hare, that's all.*

Some of the older, whiskery hares agreed with Bite-Hare, murmuring about *tricks of the light* and, *my eyes aren't what they were.* Word of Bull's dream and Mooncalf had spread far and wide, and these frail creatures could not disguise their anxiety. Run-Hare knew this.

No, she said. *I know what we saw. We all saw it. I called the names of those we had lost, and the moon showed them to us for one last, precious time.*

Run-Hare paused, and scanned the cloudless dawn, as if in the faint disappearing pinpricks of the night's stars

81

at the bluest fringes of earth's sphere, she might catch one last glimpse of the bright departed souls who had so lit up the night.

It was a sign. Our animal dreams are not just stories to scare or excite our young. They are real. They dwell beneath the ground, they float hidden in the air, they live in moonlight and fly to the stars. Which means our bull's dream is real too.

It had unexpectedly begun to patter with summer rain from a clear sky, and the hare's ears and whiskers softened in the wet, making her look more downtrodden than she felt. It was not a surprise. The sky always wept with tears when animals died – that was the animal belief.

But as she and Bite-Hare bounded back down from the Hare Circle, with the dawn chorus of blackbirds, wrens and larks summoning the day into life, despite the thickening rain, Run-Hare felt her heart rise. She felt gripped by something she had not felt since her broth-hare disappeared.

A reason to fight on.

She dared not share it with anyone, especially Bite-Hare – at least, not yet. In the dream of light in the circle, she had seen many hares lost over the last moon – trapped, hunted and poisoned.

But she had not seen the one hare she had come to mourn.

This was perhaps the greatest miracle of all that night. Little-Hare. He was still alive.

While spring had turned to summer beyond the walls of the metal box, and Run-Hare had mourned him, Little-Hare had been lost in a restless, feverish sleep, haunted by images from the bull's dream. If he wasn't being submerged under a great wet, he was fleeing wildfires. He longed to wake, but the more he tried, the deeper he sank.

The night after his sist-hare officially grieved him, he opened his eyes again. It had been a while. He twisted his head, his eyes adjusting to the light. He sniffed. He listened.

Gradually, he made sense of his surroundings. The man in the mask had gone, and the transparent worm was no longer connected to his leg. There was only a sore tingling where it had fed on his haunch. But he was still strapped down to a metal surface.

His belly spasmed with hunger, and his lips were dry and painful.

At least I'm still alive, I guess, he told himself.

The buzzard wound in his stomach was tight, but – by some moonlight miracle – it had been repaired.

Hello? he called out. *Can you at least tell me how long I've been here?*

There was no reply, and with no sight of the moon, it was impossible to tell. He felt as if he had been asleep for a very long time. Was it too late?

You don't understand. Let me out! I have to save Mooncalf!

It was no use. In the gloom of the strange dwelling, the only light came from flickering squares of human magic, and a blood-coloured glow cast across the ground. Little-Hare couldn't see much, so he decided to listen instead. He heard the constant hum of their machinery, the odd beep, and the rushes of cold air blasting down from narrow gaps in the ceiling.

Unless he found a way out, he would die here.

Bursts of panic surged through him.

His fur crawled, his legs spasmed, his eyes spun.

Little-Hare sank back against the chilly metal surface he lay on, feeling lonelier than he had ever felt in his life – which for a solitary creature such as a hare, was very lonely indeed. The human's giant box was so cold. And, as in the worst nightmares, he realised no one knew where he was.

It was odd, though, he thought, as he stared at the narrow gaps above his head, that one now had *a tail* dangling out of it, as well as cold air.

His eyes narrowed. A tail, *and* a clawed pair of feet, wriggling.

Are you just going to lie there and watch? said a deep voice from above.

Excuse me?

Nature have mercy! No time for Excuse Mes! This is not the Annual Meeting of the Polite Animal Association! Have you got paws that work or what?

Little-Hare was even more confused.

Above your head! In this human air tunnel!

Are you stuck?

No, said the voice. *I'm singing a SONG OF BEING STUCK IN AN AIR TUNNEL because I love it here so much!*

I didn't realise you were singing a song . . .

Just get ready to catch me when I jump. Ready?

Jump?

But Little-Hare didn't have time to say any more, as a harvest mouse squeezed out of the gap, in a shower of grain dust, and landed straight on his face, all scrabbling legs and whipping tail.

Help! Get off! Little-Hare protested.

The mouse did, in a single bounce. Then he picked himself up, and, standing on two legs, tapped his broad right foot.

Little-Hare couldn't help nodding up and down as

he watched.

Next, the mouse also started nodding his head, at the same time as tapping his foot. His rear waggled like a beech branch in a gale.

I'll give you a song, he said.

Little-Hare was transfixed. He didn't need or want a song. But despite his hopeless situation, he was feeling happier already. He couldn't believe his eyes when the mouse also started flexing his belly, thrusting it in and out to the same rhythm.

Ooh, yeah, ooh, yeah, he sang. *Harvest Mouse is gonna rescue the hare!*

The mouse moved faster and faster, tapping his feet, nodding his head, whipping his long tail around and around, till he was just a blur of yellowy ginger fur and claw. Harvest mice were famous in the valley for their range of dances for every emotion, but songs . . . songs were new.

I didn't know harvest mice could sing, said Little-Hare.

Just sharing the love, Little-Hare, just sharing the love, the mouse said with a chuckle. *You want more? Cos I got more, hare-baby! I got the 'Dance of No More Mice to Love'! I got 'Shake Your Tail', 'Give Me Your Heart' . . . 'This May Sound Corny, But I Love Your Ears' . . . 'Too Much Pain, Not Enough Grain' . . . 'Home is Where the Nest Is' . . . 'Feed Me Grass, Show Me Your—'*

I get the idea, thanks, said Little-Hare. *How did you get in here?*

Hey, I'm a mouse. We can get in anywhere. He sneezed, a last bit of dust from the tunnel in the ceiling.

Little-Hare was still puzzled. And just a bit suspicious. After the buzzard, and the human picking him up, his senses were on high alert. *Why? Who sent you?*

The mouse looked startled. *If that's your attitude, I'll go back just how I came in.*

He sprung off the table on to one of the metal shelf stacks of jars and bottles opposite, wrapping his tail around a strut, hauling himself back up towards the ceiling. *When you don't want me around, I'll just head back underground,* he trilled.

No! Come back! I'm sorry! Little-Hare couldn't kick anything under his straps, but if he could, he would have kicked himself. Why was he always saying the wrong thing? He wished the dream had never chosen him for this. Anyone would have been better. Even Bite-Hare.

The mouse sighed, still clinging to the shelf. *So you do want me to rescue you now?*

Yes, please, said Little-Hare in a quiet voice. *Sorry.*

No more dumb questions?

No, said the hare in an even quieter voice. *Sorry again.*

No mean wisecracks about my incredible singing?

Rescue or no rescue, Little-Hare couldn't promise this, so he just sighed in the least negative way he could manage.

The mouse leaped off the shelf, straight back on to the table, and started gnawing at the straps. *Well, if you must know,* he said, his cheeks bulging with chewed fabric, *I came because of my family. At least, the family I'm gonna have . . . *One day, my nest will be full, just like my he-a-rt!*

He chewed some more, tugging at the straps.

When I heard Bull's dream, about saving that poor mooncalf, a Terribleness coming for us all, a great wet, fires . . . Little-Hare! I cannot tell you the songs that went through my head.

Please don't share them, thought Little-Hare.

I won't share them, because . . . The harvest mouse stopped chewing and looked at Little-Hare, his eyes bright as blackcurrants. They seemed to shine and well in the low light of the cabin. *They're too sad. Although maybe just the one? 'The Tears of a Mouse'—*

It's OK. You're good, said Little-Hare.

*I don't wanna bring a nest of young mice into a world of Terribleness! What will they live on? Where will they live? How will they survive? I couldn't sleep after that. The only answer was to come down here to the farm, to find out more from the Wildness himself. That was when I saw that man pick you up. I knew straight away, from your size, that you were the one he had asked to save us . . . and I thought, *You gotta save that hare, you gotta help that hare, you gotta love that hare, because he is the one!*

Wait – when was that?

Oh . . . lemme see now. The mouse scratched his head and did some counting on his claws. *I reckon about a moon ago?*

A whole moon? Little-Hare groaned. His mistake had cost too much time already.

*Hey, don't blame me! Whoever made this strange box did not want *anything* getting in or out, without their say so. You should be happy I got here when I did, it took me for ever to chew through those pipes!*

Little-Hare couldn't speak. He didn't know what to say. He was thinking of his family. Those he had lost already. And his sist-hare, alone with Bite-Hare, after he had abandoned them. For a whole moon!

Then, they both froze. There were steps approaching outside. Human steps.

Hurry!

Yeehaw! replied the mouse, head down on to the second strap.

Little-Hare could hear someone climbing the stairs to the cabin.

Please. Quickly! he begged the mouse. Images from before flashed through his mind. The man's unblinking eyes, the sharp stabbing in his haunch, the waves of sickness that followed. *If I stay here, he'll kill me!*

The sealed door hissed open. He could hear the rain falling outside.

With a crack, the second strap snapped loose, and Little-Hare's back legs were free for the first time. They stung with pain as blood slowly returned and he flexed them. Overhead lights crackled into life. They could hear the man behind the bank of screens, removing his outer clothes, water dripping on to the floor – how wet was it outside?

Faster! begged Little-Hare, as the mouse turned to the straps on his front paws.

The mouse was chewing for his life. Then a shadow fell over them, a wave of awful human smell, and the man appeared from behind the screens. He cried in surprise, as the final strap flicked free, and the hare and the mouse jumped off the table.

Heavy booted feet fell after them –

Pushing chairs out of the way as the two animals hurtled over the smooth floor –

Their eyes rolled wildly, sniffing the air, looking for a way out –

Except there wasn't one. There were only curved corners: every crack, hole, and gap sealed with rubber. No windows, only the door the man came in through. They scrabbled, they leaped, but it was no use.

Two gloved hands lunged for them, the man cursing, as they turned back on themselves and shot between his legs.

The animals raced past the screens –

They could see the daylight squeezing through

the door, left ajar –

The rain still falling beyond, the open air, the freedom, when . . .

Little-Hare skidded to a halt.

Are you crazy? squealed the mouse. *Don't stop now, I've got an audience to wow . . .*

But Little-Hare was not listening any more. Not to the singing mouse or to the man in gloves. He was looking at the creature ahead, pale and shivering, hooked up to a mess of wires and probes, connected to beeping machines, trapped behind a plastic screen, staring straight back at him.

The creature he had been chosen by the dream to save, the creature who had brought him here in the first place. The future of the world rested on her safety.

And she was still breathing.

Mooncalf.

At the same moment, in her form on Dandelion Hill, Run-Hare awoke to find a flame dancing in the evening rain before her.

Let me protect you, my love! roared Bite-Hare, who flung himself in front of his beloved, only to get pecked on the nose for his efforts by the flame, which then spoke to him.

It is not you who needs protecting. It is our world!

The flame whirled around them, beating its wings and spraying water, before landing on the sodden ground ahead. The rain was tumbling down from the sky, harder and stronger than a whiterforce roaring over rocks.

Excuse me? said Run-Hare, still trying to work out who or what was speaking to her. *Do we know you?*

What does that matter? said the flame. *The only

thing you need to know is that it is not too late to save the mooncalf and stop the Terribleness. But you are not going to stop anything by sleeping in your hole!*

Run-Hare blinked herself awake, and now saw that the speaker was not a flame, but a young waxwing, with a reddish crest, her yellow wing tips and pale belly still bright under the streaks of rain.

Shouldn't you have flown back home by now? said Run-Hare.

No! Not yet. My message is too important.

A message for who?

YOU! What are you going to do?

Bite-Hare drew himself up to his full height, blustering. *Now listen here, I don't know who you think you are, young bird, but you can't just turn up out of the blue, and start telling us all what to do—*

*So we don't all die? Yes, that is exactly what I *can* do, and moreover I *must*!*

Somehow, the way she spoke, the intensity of her message, left the hares mesmerised.

What . . . do you want us to do? said Run-Hare.

Waxwing thought for a moment, cocking her head. *Your broth-hare is missing, along with Mooncalf. So perhaps we need to find them.*

We have looked everywhere!

Pah! said the bird. *You haven't even started. No, to

stop a Terribleness requires more than sniffing a few weeds. Did you hear the bull's dream or not? We have had omens! The white falling out of winter! There will be a great wet, fires . . .*

I heard, said Run-Hare, now wide awake, as the power of the spiralling, fiery animal vision at the Hare Circle raced through her again.

Dreams are real.

So you know what is coming! Yes, we don't know where the humans are keeping Mooncalf. Yes, your broth-hare has disappeared looking for her. Does that mean we just give up and go back to sleep?

Well, now you come to mention it— said Bite-Hare, yawning.

And just let the Terribleness destroy the world? Of course not! So now, you must ORGANISE!

Organise? said Bite-Hare, who did not generally like to organise much more than where the next mouthful of dandelion leaves was coming from.

Organise, repeated Run-Hare thoughtfully.

ORGANISE! Stop feeling sorry for yourselves, gather this wild of yours together and work as a team to save Mooncalf.

But other animals never listen to hares, said Bite-Hare. *They don't trust us.*

Then that is their problem. If they don't, they will perish along with every creature that has ever lived, said Waxwing and with a flap of her wings, she disappeared back into the pouring rain, a fast-receding ball of righteous fire.

*

In the low electric light of the Facto cabin, no one had spoken at all after the discovery of Mooncalf. The hare and the mouse stared at the calf in astonishment, while the man carefully closed the cabin door.

The rain drumming on the roof was so close that for a moment, Little-Hare was outside in the wild again, free, shivering under a grey sky. But he wasn't, and the noise made it hard to think. Was that a distant rumble of thunder?

He made himself as small and low as he could against the floor, watchful as ever. There were none of the things he normally watched for here, though – the soaring wing of a rook, the flash of a fox tail, tips of corn shuddering in the sun –

Mouse broke his daydream with a song, as he gazed at the silvery white calf in wonder. *It's never too late to rescue you, never gonna give up on you, never gonna leave without you—*

Yes, Mooncalf, said Little-Hare. *Mouse is right. We're not giving up without a fight.*

It might have been a trick of the light, but Mooncalf's eyes seemed to brim with water at this, then she turned away from them as much as she could, her whole body hooked and wired to monitors and drips. Her body seemed even more silvery and thinner than before. She didn't say a word. She never did.

It's all right. I understand. You don't need to speak, because you're a mooncalf, Little-Hare murmured in wonder. He wanted to reach out and touch her.

I'm afraid the mouse is wrong, said the man behind them. *It is too late.*

His words sent tremors of confusion through Little-Hare's skull again. A human talking in their tongue! The unique animal voice that only beasts of the wild understood and heard in their heads. It was wrong, it was weird, it made him want to run far, far away, where he would never hear it ever again.

But there was no way in or out of the cabin. They were trapped against the plastic curtains, cowering as the man approached, his shadow looming over them.

Why . . . can I understand your words? said Little-Hare.

The man squatted down to face them at eye-level. This was it, Little-Hare felt sure now – the end. Slaughtered by a human in this unnatural box stinking of their magic. He had failed the bull, failed them all. Again.

He tried to fight it, but he couldn't.

The man, the walls of the cabin dissolved, and in his mind, he was back there, moons ago, in the Wheat Between the Woods –

The bars of summer evening light, the blur of wheat

tips in his eyes, he had been playing with Run-Hare in among the crop. Nibbling some food here, chasing a butterfly there, mock-boxing each other, tumbling over in the sun.

Then out of nowhere, Moth-hare and Fath-hare, hurtling over the horizon, screaming at them.

Then, what happened next –

He shook his head.

Their final moments were a blank to him. How could he ask Run-Hare? What would she think of him – not even remembering how their own kin were lost?

Little-Hare just knew that meant it was his fault.

It had to be.

By the time Run-Hare reached the bottom of the hill, the rain had gathered and swelled into a downpour that blotted out what remained of the light, and flattened the green, running so heavy and fast down her head that she could only just see.

The sheep had retreated to the shelter of their old oak, shivering under its dripping spread. They gathered around a bale of straw slowly shedding its strands over the slushy green. Everything was sodden. Was that water seeping up from the ground now as well as the sky? Something very strange was happening to Dandelion Hill.

Run-Hare shook the distracting thoughts away as she approached the ram and ewe who guided this flock. But before she could even say a word, Ewe got in first.

Don't! I know what you've come about. The bull's dream? It was you hares that got him started on all this, we heard.

Run-Hare darted around them. *So will you help me save Mooncalf and stop the Terribleness?*

It certainly makes you think, admitted Ewe.

Think! We've all got to do more than think, said Run-Hare, trying to summon the urgency of the waxwing. *The Terribleness is due by Cow Moon, if we don't save the calf. So you can't just . . . stand here and munch the green all sun long!*

The sheep thought hard for a moment.

That is . . . literally . . . what sheep are meant to do, said Ram.

Then the sheep thought hard for another moment.

I know! said the ewe brightly. *We'll all eat a little less green each day. Not much, just a little less green.*

How in the name of all beasts will that help save Mooncalf, you daft ewe? said Ram.

We are sheep, dear Ram! There are a limited number of ways in which we can help our fellow creatures. We can eat more green, if there is too much, or eat less, if there is not enough. So just to make sure there is plenty of fresh green for Mooncalf, when you do save her, we won't eat it all. Yet.

Their flock bleated in approval. Run-Hare shifted about on the wet ground, now more mud than green. Was this rain ever going to stop? It didn't just fall from the sky, it hammered and exploded and drenched. This was not the sky weeping tears at the death of an animal, but more a full-blown tantrum, tipping all the water there was down upon their heads.

Ram nodded, spraying droplets into the air. *Very well, Hare, you have our answer. We, the sheep, of Old Farm, vow to eat a little less green every day, to help save the mooncalf, as commanded by the bull's dream.*

Run-Hare had to be careful. *That is very wise of you both, Ram and Ewe, and good of you too, good of *all* sheep. But . . .*

Oh, no! said the ram. *Typical hare. There's always a but.*

Never satisfied, are they? said the ewe.

No, I am very satisfied, thank you, she said. *But what about finding Mooncalf? Where do you think she might be?*

What about finding her? We're doing our bit! said the ram. *You can't go round attacking animals who do their bit.* He stuck his face right in hers. *You hares think you're so special, don't you? With your long legs, your bright eyes and your cleverness. You're no better than us!*

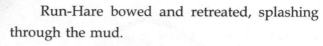

Run-Hare bowed and retreated, splashing through the mud.

Organising other creatures was hard. It was going to take time; she saw that now. She glanced up at the dulled light of the Hare Moon, only just visible through the slicing rain and clumps of furious cloud. A moon that was already beginning to change.

Time was the one thing she didn't have.

Don't be . . . scared, said the man to Little-Hare.

Wow! said the mouse. *A talking human! That is so cool and *inspiring*.*

Please don't start singing again, though, said Little-Hare, gritting his teeth.

Hey, Mr Man-imal, his companion crooned, clicking his tiny claws as he swayed. *You talk like an ani-mal!*

I do! said the man. And for the first time, the hare noticed that his eyes were softer and kinder than he had first thought. The curls which peeked out from under the cap on his head were the colour of sand. *I don't yet . . . understand why. I think it's . . . a family thing. But that's not important right now . . . Perhaps I should begin by telling you my name? Dawson Jaynes. I'm a professor, you see. I work for the, ah, food company which owns this . . . farm. Factorium Foods.*

Both the animals, who lived in a world of air and green and blood, let the words *work* and *company* float meaninglessly over their heads.

I'm their vet . . . trained to look after animals. You have to, ah, trust me. This calf is not . . . well, she's very sick indeed.

She looks OK to me, said the harvest mouse, who was not a vet.

Professor Jaynes sighed. *I wish she was, but we need to do more . . . tests, that kind of thing. There's a process happening that we don't . . . it appears she is burning up.*

Burning up?

It started with a fever . . . when we found her, said the professor.

Actually, I found her, said Little-Hare. *I've been chosen.*

I know. I saw you that night. That's why I've kept you . . . for so long . . . even after stitching up that wound . . . You've been in, ah, quarantine.

Quarantine? Another meaningless human word.

The professor looked at the floor and wrung his gloved hands. Suddenly he was less frightening, just tired and worried. *I think it's . . . a virus. None of the usual medicines seem to . . . you know. It's one of the most powerful pathogens we've ever . . . and it's spreading

103

through her system very slowly . . . determined to destroy every bit, you see.*

The rain pounded the roof of the cabin, trying to punch a way in. Storm winds rattled the door, as if it might be wrenched free at any moment.

Little-Hare looked the man dead in the eye, and the man had never been looked in the eye before by a hare. It was an ancient, unblinking stare that saw through humans and their machines and clothes and words like *quarantine* and *pathogen*, and saw the animal of flesh and hair and skin and bone underneath.

The professor sighed. *If the virus in this calf escapes and spreads, then . . . well . . . catastrophe. It could kill hundreds, thousands of animals. In this valley and beyond. A plague!*

Mooncalf hung her head. Cows were used to awful things happening to them, but she had no instincts to prepare her for this. The harvest mouse, for once, fell silent at the thought too.

Little-Hare would not hang his head, though. He would not be silenced. Not any more. He would make up for what happened in the wheat open last summer. For at last, a dreadful realisation had seeped through his veins, drenching the very core of his understanding.

Not many of these human words made any sense to him. But there was one word which did, the only word which possibly struck more fear in any living animal than fire.

He now knew what the Terribleness was, that he had to save Mooncalf to prevent.

But chosen or not, how on earth could he? For it was terrible indeed.

It was worse than even the greatest of wets, or the wildest of fires.

The death of thousands of wild creatures.

A *plague*.

Run-Hare sprinted to the fenced paddock. Horses had stopped working the land long before her great-grand-hare's time, but one of their smaller cousins still lived here, because she provided entertainment for the farmer's she-child, who liked to ride her. To all in the valley, she was known as Pretty Pony.

Oh, dear, sweet hare! Pretty Pony called out, with a flick of her perfectly groomed and ribboned tail, as she watched Run-Hare approach through the sheets of rain. *I think it's so marvellous what you are doing, trying to help that poor mooncalf. I could not be more behind you.*

Run-Hare placed her paws on the slippery bars of Pretty Pony's gate. *So *you* will help me find and save her!*

Pretty chewed some fresh hay with a thoughtful look. *As you know, my she-child owner often takes me to human ceremonies – where they make me ride around, jump over things and do silly tricks. It's very tedious, but there are always lots of humans there pointing their

105

flashing boxes at me. A kind of modest fame, I suppose . . .*

Run-Hare cocked her ears, confused. *And . . . how will that help save Mooncalf, Pretty?*

I will draw attention to your cause! I guarantee my influencing skills will bring Mooncalf unprecedented awareness and fame!

Run-Hare sighed and crept away, her ears flattened by the downpour. *What are you going to do?* Waxwing had challenged her. Not: *Who are you going to influence?*

Her ears fell lower and flatter as she crept around the farmyard. The goats shied away in their pen even as they saw her coming.

You are unlucky, hare! Stay away, warned old Billy Goat, who was so white, grave and ancient that he could have been wearing human eyeglasses. *We do not want to get involved with your calf. Farm animals like us are put on this earth for one reason only. If we don't let ourselves be milked, and sheared, and killed on the scale we have grown used to, the humans will grow weak. This farm, our kind's dwelling for many moons, will fail.*

Everywhere Run-Hare ran, it was the same, the rain pounding harder and harder, till she felt more water than hare. Even the cows, the bull's own herd, barely lifted their shaggy heads from the troughs of feed in front of their cages.

Have no fear. Mooncalf will be saved by human magic. Have faith in magical solutions! Our human masters make shelters that stop rain, build walk-upons over fish-roads and ride in machines – their magic can save any creature and stop any Terribleness!

The pigs dismissed the whole dream as a pile of manure.

A conspiracy theory, they said, *invented by Bull and his cows just so they can get more food than us. Mooncalf is fine. There is no Terribleness! It's a fake dream!*

The rain came down, harder and faster, turning the ground into a swamp. There was a distant rumble that must have been thunder, but it seemed to come from within the hill itself, deep beneath Run-Hare's feet. She felt the weight of the sky upon her, soaking and pushing her into the ground as she limped back to her form.

It was useless. Everything was hopeless.

Why have you left me, Little-Hare? Where are you? Not one other creature will help me. She gazed up at the sky, but if the Hare Moon was still there, it was obliterated from view by storm clouds and rain. She cried out all the same. *Help me! I cannot stop a Terribleness on my own!*

The same rain beat down ever faster on the metal roof of the cabin. And there was another sudden booming rumble. That had to be thunder, Little-Hare was sure of it. It was very loud and very close.

You keep saying We, he said to the man. *Who is We?*

Factorium! said the professor. *Factorium, er, Foods. Or Facto . . .*

So that's what that stupid word means. Little-Hare snorted. He imagined that when humans talked about food, dead animals were never far behind in the conversation. *You just want to make Mooncalf better so then you can kill her and eat her.*

The rumbling was now so loud the professor had to raise his voice to be heard.

*Never! I'm a scientist . . . I've spent my whole life . . . caring for animals. I work for Facto because they can imagine a future where humans don't depend on animals for food, you see? At least . . . some people there do . . . I was here, in this mobile lab, doing research into different

108

kinds of food we might grow or even make . . . when we discovered this calf.*

Little-Hare was not convinced. He thought of Buzzard. All animals, including humans, never changed their nature quickly or easily.

Then why don't you and this . . . Facto . . . leave this problem to us?

Professor Jaynes glanced down, his face softening.

*Because I'm not just a scientist . . . I have a family. I'm a . . . father. If this virus spreads . . . if it jumps from animals to humans . . . I want to make sure our son has, you know, a *future*.*

Little-Hare began to understand. *You have a he-child?*

The man smiled properly for the first time, a faraway look in his eyes. *Yes. I have great hopes for him. He already, ah, likes animals as much as me . . . but he's so young. He hardly knows this wonderful world yet. I want him to have a chance to experience it.*

For the first time, the hare saw real emotion in the professor's face. He saw all the fear, all the worry, all the love that he felt and more. It was a strange thing to do, perhaps, but it happened so instinctively, there was no time to think. He had lost a fath-hare. No one should have to lose a son. Not even a human.

*Very well, then. *Professor*.* The word was so odd, but he liked the sound of it. Little-Hare held out a single paw. *Will you help us save Mooncalf and stop the Terribleness – for your son?*

The man's grip was gentle and warm.

We can try, Little-Hare. I hope you'll meet him one day. His name is Kester. Kester Jaynes.

When Run-Hare finally climbed back into her form the following morning, weary and sodden, she was too dejected to notice that the rain was getting even stronger, or that it still showed no signs of stopping.

Rivulets of muddy water swept down the hill, over, under and past her. They channelled into the earth, which seemed to be on the move itself, the strange cracks widening into messy gulfs as the water muddied them. Nor did she notice the tall-homes and telegraph poles at the top of the hill slowly list to one side, as the ground started running away from them.

She couldn't sleep. All she could do was stare into space. Her fur was sodden, her teeth chattering, and who cared, what did any of that matter any more?

No one even knew where Mooncalf was, never mind

how to save her. That meant a Terribleness was coming. Perhaps this rain was the beginning. Perhaps it had started already. Bull said the dream foretold a great wet as one of the signs.

Her pleas to the wild for help had fallen on deaf ears. It was funny how so many animals acted as if they cared about their wild, but when you asked them to help, they stuck to their own old ways, behaving just as they always had. It was as if each animal had developed over time to behave only in their own particular way, always to their own advantage – as if none of the animals felt that saving Mooncalf was *their* problem to share.

It won't affect us, someone else will save her, and we're all going to die anyway – those were the phrases she had heard over and over again, from farmyard to forest.

As night blurred into dawn, she found herself lost in these grim and gloomy thoughts. Her mind retreated in on itself, a frightened creature burrowing deeper and deeper into a subterranean network of endless, lightless tunnels. So she didn't notice Bite-Hare at first, nudging her with his nose.

Go away, you lump! She scowled. *It's no use, just leave me alone. The sheep are right, they're *all* right, what good can any of us do?*

I know you are downcast, light of my life, but—

I said, go away and leave me alone! Or do you want me to make you?

She bared her teeth and prepared to strike. Bite-Hare

shrank back. *But, my eternal apple of love, it is not I who has come to see you!*

What do you mean?

Run-Hare sat up in her form, shaking the worst of the wet away, even though it continued to fall, drumming on her head and whiskers. Bite-Hare slid back over the slippery green to reveal who her visitor – or rather, she saw now, *visitors* were.

The rain sluiced over her eyes. A new day was only just beginning, and at first it was hard to make the figures out in the watery gloom. But then the black storm clouds which had been massing overhead suddenly rumbled with rage, sending a fork of light down out of the sky, and the shadowy shapes gathered around her were lit up in a flash.

It was the young ones.

A lamb, a kid goat and a young chick led the group of animal young, which also included piglets and a wobbly foal. From the woods there were fox and badger cubs, and some small hedgerow bird fledglings of various varieties pecked over the ground. They should have been with their parents, in their pens, setts or nests.

But they weren't, they were here. And not alone, either – the young waxwing hovered behind them, like a flaming halo.

What do you want? Run-Hare said, perplexed.

The lamb spoke first, stepping forward, her wool shimmering with bright beads of water. She looked worried. *We were listening when you spoke to our ram

113

and ewe.* The lamb chewed her bottom lip.
Can I let you in on a secret?

Be my guest, said Run-Hare.

I love my mum and dad, said Lamb, *but . . .*

Your secret is safe with me, I promise.

Sometimes they drive me mad!

They never think! added the kid goat, pawing the ground.

Then all the young animals were shouting at once.

All they do is drift about eating green all day long!

They'll do whatever humans tell them to do!

They just want everything to stay the same!

The only visitor who hadn't spoken was the young chick. Now he pecked forward. He was very unusual looking. There was something scatty about his appearance, even for a chick in the pouring rain, as if every feather was simultaneously facing in the wrong direction from its neighbour.

*Run-Hare, * he said. *I spend most of my day pecking at things, for no reason. It is a fact universally acknowledged that I am the stupidest chick on the farm, if not the whole world. All the others call me Stupid Chick.*

We do, confirmed the kid goat, nodding.

But even I, said Stupid Chick, his head bobbing up and down, *the stupidest chick in the universe, can see that if our own leader, Bull, says that unless we save Mooncalf, there is a Terribleness coming – maybe we should do something about it!*

And once we heard that, said Kid Goat, *we all agreed with Waxwing to come and see you, Run-Hare.*

Why? What do you want me to do?

WHAT DO YOU THINK? cried Waxwing in exasperation. *Lead them! Organise, like I said!*

Why me, though?

Waxwing says not all of us are natural leaders, said Stupid Chick, slipping over in some mud on to his beak. *And we are younger than you.*

*I don't know if I am a natural leader either, * said Run-Hare, gently helping Stupid Chick up again. *I lost Little-Hare, and I couldn't convince any of your elders to follow me.*

The disappointment of her visitors hung heavy and silent in the relentless rain splashing over them.

Looking around for some way to fill this void, Bite-Hare spied a shaft of early morning light that briefly broke through the clouds. In the same beam of sun he also glimpsed a different future for himself. He had long since realised that he could not beat Run-Hare in a fight. She had resisted his every attempt to make her fall in love with him.

There was one last idea.

Perhaps, he could prove himself to her? In the service of a cause she believed in! Now that irritating young broth-hare of hers was gone, he would run to her rescue, and that of the whole wild. He would show her what a strong and noble mate he could be.

The dawn light moved off over the hills, and the morning turned dark once more, as did his gaze. He showed his teeth as he raised a front paw to the assembled young.

I shall lead you all! he said suddenly, with a glint in his eye. He rose on his back legs, punching the air with his paws, as thunder boomed across the valley. Again, the noise sounded like it came from beneath their feet as much as the sky. *You are all so brave to leave your elders and come here at some risk to yourselves. Your bravery will not be in vain. I . . . Bite-Hare the Brave, will lead you!*

Bite-Hare the Brave? said Run-Hare incredulously. *Get real.*

We will find and save Mooncalf! We will stop the Terribleness! His heart pumped, and he felt blood rushing to his head. *All those who do not join us, or are against us, are against the wild! They must perish! Who is with me?*

But his question was never answered.

Whatever the young had imagined the hares would do for them, whatever Waxwing had hoped Run-Hare would organise, whatever hare-brained scheme Bite-Hare had half dreamed up, they all had one unfortunate fact in common.

116

They were too late.

Much, much too late.

The mysterious cracks in the ground and buildings, the unexpected water springs, the lopsided tall-homes – these had all been warning signs, but no one had noticed.

For years, the soil had been eroded by wind and rain and over-farming, but the humans had not done anything. Many of the tall-homes or hedges which might have helped block any earth movement had been felled or ripped up to create more and more space for human food. And now, late, heavy falls of white followed by torrential rain had loosened the ground beyond repair.

So whatever any animal had to say in reply was lost, as the top of Dandelion Hill collapsed in on itself.

It was the loudest, most deafening sound the wild had ever heard. A vast, ricocheting boom crashed, as the great boulders of the Hare Circle, on the hill top above, began to move.

Bite-Hare felt the ground shake under his feet. *What is going on?*

Stupid Chick cried out, pointing a wing behind him. *Look! The rocks are coming! Down the hill towards us!*

*Must you be so stupid *all* the time?* said Bite-Hare, and then there was a horrendous, slithering roar –

The boulders did not travel alone.

They surfed on a thundering, churning tide of mud, stone and green that engulfed everything in its way.

The hares ran as fast as they had ever run in their

lives, the young animals scattering, stumbling and screaming as they went, trying to outrun the hill. Waxwing flew away, trying to find a tall-home that still stood to perch on.

Follow me! yelled Run-Hare to Bite-Hare, as the muddy deluge licked at their paws.

I'm trying, my love, said Bite-Hare, panting for breath just behind her. *But you're so fast—*

The muddy wave rose up fast and devoured those that could not run or fly away quickly enough. They were turned over and over, they hit the ground, each other, soil choking their nostrils, filling their mouths, blinding their eyes, as the landslide dragged them down the hill towards the farm. A slithering pile of belching mud that grew and grew with a fetid, slurping roar as it slid into the first barn on the edge of the complex.

Not far away, in the tiny metal cabin, after a long night of discussion, Professor Jaynes reached his conclusion. *To stay safe . . . don't go outside. Shelter here . . . The calf's infection will develop, and then spread. So we will keep testing, researching and in time, develop a cure. * He paused. *What's that noise?*

The thunder was now so loud and so close that Little-Hare couldn't hear himself think. Professor Jaynes reached for the door. Just as he did, Little-Hare's long hare ears detected what the thunder actually was.

It wasn't thunder at all.

Don't! he screamed.

But he was too late. The man grabbed the handle –

There was the rubble, mud and turf, all in a wave –

Little-Hare was sent head over heels. He felt the mouse grab his tail with his claws. Was that the man screaming?

Mooncalf? he called out, and then he couldn't speak any more. He didn't have time to think, either. Muddy brown water surged through the door of the cabin, turning it over and over, a great rattle of gushing liquid –

Little-Hare tried to see. He tried to breathe. He tried to swim –

But the power of the water, the force of the slippage was too great.

He could do only one thing, as his world went liquid and dark.

Give in.

How Run-Hare could breathe, she did not know. She had been terrified she might never breathe again. Clotted brown water had filled her throat and ears, till she was more liquid than animal. Rising up, she had gasped for air –

Only to duck a branch, swinging towards her –

Plunged down against a rock, reeling off again –

Her ears full of the muffled underwater cries of those swept up alongside –

And then, silence and darkness fell.

But now she felt cool air on her back, and wet ground beneath her belly. She cracked open one eye for a chink of grey daylight. Every bone, every muscle ached. Her tongue found a dribble of dried blood on her muzzle. Wincing, she dared to move, and found that she could, even if every limb of her own body felt like a fur sack full of rocks.

She tried to piece together, in her muddled mind, what had brought her here in such a state. It had been so sudden, swift and brutal. And now, the world was quiet and calm again, eerily so. The morning that had begun with her home exploding into a slithering surge of mud and water, was now just another chilly early summer's day in the valley.

As she slowly opened her eyes and tried to make sense of where she was, she found her world so transformed and unfamiliar that at first she feared she had crossed over to the Great Beyond. She was sprawled on top of a kind of mound.

It all made sense now. The cracks at the top of the hill, and in the bull's dwelling. The unexplained springs of water beneath the sheep's oak. The lopsided tall-homes. Dandelion Hill had been collapsing for moons, and trying to warn them, but they hadn't listened.

A great wet.

Bull's dream had warned about water covering the earth – was this the Terribleness it had warned about? Or just a sign of it? In any case, it had brought her to the human dwelling.

Where there had been farm tracks, there was now a filthy, low, muddy stretch of liquid that did not flow like a fish-road, but wallowed between the remains of buildings, half-submerged walls and hedges.

A dreadful stink shimmered over everything, of mess and bodies. In the water, things floated, things that she did not want to think too much about. The dawn chorus today was a disjointed series of cries for help from humans and beasts, isolated wails coming from those trapped in or under wreckage.

What more was to come? Her thoughts were interrupted by the robin, perched on a crooked telegraph pole, that was entangled in fallen wires, calling out, *Final warning! When I find out who did this, they are going to pay! Big time!*

Run-Hare stirred herself into life and on to her feet. She was knocked and torn, and so wet she thought she might never feel dry again.

A little trail of dandelions, uprooted and lifeless, wound their way down to the water, where hundreds floated, as if the stars had fallen out of the sky.

And there, face down among them in the stagnant stream, was a furry mound.

Another hare!

She limped down her rubbish mountain as fast as she could, trying to avoid curls of rusting barbed wire, jagged edges and sharp rocks.

Little-Hare! she cried. *My broth-hare! I knew you weren't gone; I'm coming for you.* Laughing and sobbing at the same time, she crouched on a rock, and pawed at the water, trying to drag the mound towards her. *Come on!*

For every lunge, the hare seemed to spin out of reach –

Then, at last, she hooked him in, pulling him towards her –

The mound rolled over, spluttered, and scrambled ashore in a panic.

She stepped back in horror.

My love, my rescuer! said Bite-Hare, sounding not quite right. *Praise the moon that you survived. I knew you would save me!*

He shook himself as dry as he could, picking out burrs and berries from his sodden fur. Then he glanced in the water and saw what had caused Run-Hare to recoil in the first place. Bite-Hare stared at his reflection . . . and slowly put his paw to his mouth.

His whiskers were broken and bent, his ears flopped forlornly down the side of his head, and where there had once been the two largest front teeth ever seen on a hare, there was now just a bloodied, black gap.

My teeth, he murmured, touching the empty gums gingerly. Then, with a scream of rage, the first time he had ever truly disturbed Run-Hare, echoing around the watery wastes: *My teeth!*

Run-Hare felt a ripple of feeling she never expected to have for this hare.

He was hurt, and more than that, he looked so wretched and reduced. Not a threat to anything. She tried to comfort him. *They must have been knocked out as we tumbled through the wet. Perhaps a branch, a fence post, a rock . . .

You will recover. You must rest. I once had an old grandfath-hare with only one tooth, and he ate perfectly—*

His body froze, rigid with rage. *And I say, with my remaining teeth, the truth.* He looked again at the water, touching his lips over and over again, as if it would somehow make the reflection different. Sobs shuddered through his battered, damp body. *This *was* the Terribleness! Don't you see? It came for *me*! I am cursed. Doomed never to love, never to be loved.*

Bite-Hare! When will you realise that this isn't all about you? Besides, it doesn't make any difference to me whether you have two front teeth or none. That's not how I think of my fellow creatures. It's who you are and what you do that counts.

Don't lie! He shrank away from her. *You never loved me –* he glanced again at his reflection in the filthy water – *and now you never will!*

Run-Hare looked around them and saw human furniture, carved of wood, bobbing along, and the tops of human farm machines poking out of the water, like metal beetle shells. *I know it seems crazy, but I still believe that somewhere, Mooncalf is out there. We have till Cow Moon. Midsummer. It's not long, but we can still stop the Terribleness. I don't think this was it. Just a sign that one is coming if we don't do something.*

Bite-Hare looked at her, unable to speak. He waved his paws about in confusion, and then suddenly, there was that familiar flash of cunning in his bruised eyes, the gift every hare-brain was blessed with, for good or bad. And he started to laugh.

His laugh was sickly and frightening. He roared so much that he rolled on to his side in the mud, clutching his belly. *Stop the Terribleness?* He tossed a paw at the devastation simmering around them. *Don't you think it's a little late for that?*

Somewhere in what remained of the opens behind them, a couple of rooks cawed to each other. There were some distant shouts and a splash near the farmhouse. Then silence again, just the dirty, oily water lapping at the edge of the mud mountain.

My moth-hare once told me, said Run-Hare slowly, *that it was never too late. It is never too late to keep on running, living and hoping. Do you

know when she told me that? When she lay dying in the wheat open last summer. Her final gift. The most important thing she ever told me were her very last words. It is never too late.*

Bite-Hare clapped his paws together, and rubbed them briskly, as if he was wiping them clean of some filth. *As it happens, *my love,* I couldn't disagree more. This is more than a *sign*! The Terribleness has happened. You have lost your broth-hare and I have lost my teeth. Look around you! It is very much too late for many of us.*

Run-Hare's ears had some water in them, but there was no mistaking his words. *Thinking like that will get us nowhere.*

Bite-Hare shivered. The wind blowing off the wet was bitter, cutting through both of them. *You've never liked me, have you, Run-Hare?*

That's not fair.

You think I'm a fool, I know. You and your little broth-hare, conspiring behind my back. I heard you. Old Bite-Hare with his grinding teeth, and now his . . . gap. Enjoying every chance you got to beat me up.

I just . . . I don't know if you're the right mate for me, that's all. But I do know that out there, somewhere, is the right jill-hare for you.

Then something happened which Run-Hare would regret for the rest of her life. She happened to notice a curled-up dandelion stuck on top of Bite-Hare's matted head, the muddied gold just catching the light.

Suddenly, it was all too much.

This sodden and angry hare, fur all rubbed the wrong way, his toothless mouth contrasting with his furious gaze, the little flower stranded comically between his ears, crusted with mud – all her worry and stress about her broth-hare and the bull's dream and the great wet came out in the worst way possible.

Somehow, for the first time ever, he almost – looked adorable.

And she laughed.

Immediately, she realised her mistake. *I'm sorry, Bite-Hare,* she said hastily. *I don't mean to, I'm not laughing at you, only there's this dandelion on your head—*

With a paw, she stretched to flick it away, but he recoiled, as if she was boxing him once more. He was not smiling. In silence, he turned his back on her, and hopped back down to the edge of the rubbish pile till the dirty waves lapped at his paws.

Come back! she called. *I'm sorry, I didn't mean it . . .*

Bite-Hare turned around one last time. His voice was the most solemn she had ever heard him. No more wooing or acting. For once, it sounded like he was speaking the truth of his hare-heart, and it sliced straight through hers. *You will be sorry for the day you laughed at me.* He glared at the simmering wet and silent dwellings. *You all will be.*

And he sprang into the foul water, swimming away from her with hard, defiant strokes.

Little-Hare was cold.

He was also damp, bruised and frightened. But he was still alive. It was that thought that kept him running alongside a stumbling, sick calf, as they tried to make their way up the remaining side of Dandelion Hill through a waterlogged Ash Wood.

His bedraggled hare-head spun on the inside with so many questions.

How could that human speak the sacred animal tongue? How would he now stop the Terribleness, this plague that burned Mooncalf up from the inside? And worst of all, why had he been stuck with an endlessly singing mouse as his companion?

It's just one step in front of anoth-hare, trilled Harvest Mouse, *for one brave calf and the guy I call broth-hare!*

128

Little-Hare swerved ahead, up the wooded slope, scouting for drier land, leaping over moss-fringed pools and scrabbling along muddy tracks. Mooncalf trailed along behind him, the mouse sitting on her head, singing away as if nothing had happened. As if they hadn't all just nearly drowned in a great wet, battered by rocks and tumbling fence posts, water filling their gullets, paws and hooves flailing.

The wet had turned the human box over and over, like a hollow log bumping down a whiterforce, filling with wet. Then it was dragged over some sharp farm machinery, tearing it open, letting the liquid out and the air in. The two smaller animals had clambered on to one of the ragged edges, clinging for life, Mooncalf sprawled in a corner, until finally, the great wet hit an unmovable barn wall of metal, its journey over.

Little-Hare had lost sight of the human. Had he escaped, or been swept under?

Professor Jaynes.

He had talked to them of *viruses*, of *therapies*, of *tests* . . . but all these strange words felt a world away, scattered with the rest of the rubbish the landslide had spread over Old Farm below. Behind him, Mooncalf paused in between the mouse's verses, her breathing heavy. Each gasp was a shudder, every exhalation a wince.

Little-Hare didn't turn around or speak to her, because he knew if he did, Mooncalf might see the fear in his hare-eyes, hear the worry in his voice. They were going to higher and drier ground, but that alone would not make her better.

Finally, the tall-homes thinned out, revealing the wall that bordered Ash Wood, and a gateway leading to a wheat open. An army of green, faceless upright stalks greeted them, casting spiky shadows over the earth as the day ended. They were beginning to form ears on their tips, but the crop was bent and flattened in patches from the storm.

Opposite was another woodland, small and shady, where badgers built their setts, and foxes dug their dens in between the heavy roots. Much to the foxes' fury, this was officially known as Badger Beech Copse.

Little-Hare paused in the gateway, his claws slicing into the wet earth. He had not been to this open since last summer. But now he had no choice. He took a deep breath. *This place is special to me. The Wheat Between Woods.*

There is nothing more neat, howled Harvest Mouse, *than foraging in wheat*! Oh, yeah! This will also be a perfect place for my new nest.* With a whoop, he slid down the calf's side, and trotted off to explore. Mooncalf looked as if she might melt with exhaustion at any moment. She could barely stand.

Come on, said Little-Hare. *I know a quiet spot where you will be out of sight.*

He slipped through the stalks, the calf hobbling after as best she could, the harvest mouse whistling yet another melody to himself as he scurried alongside. At last, Little-Hare flopped down, in the middle of the open, only the very tops of his ears visible among the wheat tips. Mooncalf lowered herself next to him with care, flattening a circle of crops as she did.

Little-Hare gazed out into the valley below, the full and overflowing fish-road surging along through it, a course it had ploughed long before any of the animals of Dandelion Hill came into the world. As the sun sank in the sky, the water flashed silver, the dusky heavens twinkled with bright stars, and the three animals watched as a noisy flock of starlings drew their dark glittering veil across the sunset in bold, sweeping strokes. The great wet had destroyed so much, but the world found a way to carry on.

This valley was all he had known his entire life.

It seemed impossible to imagine Dandelion Hill without starlings in the sky, or butterflies dancing in the flowers, yet that was what the Terribleness threatened, according to the bull's dream – now confirmed by the human professor. He looked down at his paws.

He had known change already, of course. In this very open, not even twelve moons ago. Trapped between two woods, difficult for humans to reach, it had been one of the safest places in the valley for hares.

He had not wanted to remember before, he couldn't take the pain.

But now, here again, sitting in the exact same spot, inhaling the same sweet, drowsy summer scent again, bathed in the same soft light, the memories came rushing back, whether he wanted them to or not.

Run-Hare had arrived first that balmy evening, followed by him. They had nibbled, and chased, and batted butterflies with their paws. Then Fath-hare and Moth-hare had burst into view, their greying ear tips jagging through the wheat. And not far behind, their hunters.

Dog, Lurcher and Hound, trampling the crop as they surrounded their quarry.

He had been making Run-Hare laugh. A somersault. Plunging into the crop and reappearing with a worm balanced on his nose. Now, suddenly, his beloved hare-kin were screaming at him to run, do something, anything to distract the dogs, as their strength began to fade . . .

But he hadn't.

Little-Hare had sat rooted to the spot, paralysed by fear, as hares and rabbits sometimes are, even as death howled and consumed them right in front of him, even as Run-Hare tried to draw the hunters off –

He could have acted, but he didn't.

And now they were gone, for ever.

His fault! For being silly when the world was always a dangerous place. For not warning them soon enough.

For failing to act when he could and should have.

For failing them all.

Little-Hare looked around, worry etched into the tight lines that wrinkled over his fur. It was night, and for a moment, all was silent in the wheat open. Mooncalf and Harvest Mouse were dozing next to him, and he felt very alone. He eyed the pale Hare Moon that had guided so many hares before him.

Some said it was possible to see hares in the moon, if the light was right. That when hares travelled to the Great Beyond, that was where their spirits flew up to, to live for eternity. Had Run-Hare now been sent there too by the great wet?

He wondered if any of his ancestors were up there listening.

For he had never needed a miracle more than tonight.

Oh, Fath-hare and Moth-hare! I'm sorry I couldn't save you. But now I have to stop a Terribleness all by myself. And I don't know if I can.

It was hard to say if it was an answer from the moon or not, but as he made this call, a low, silvery breath crept over the ground. Soft and damp, it spread along the hill, covering the crops, the animals slumbering by him, veiling the woods and walls, filling the valley with clouds of sparkling mist.

Suddenly he couldn't see anything.

Was this the plague? Had it come already?

His heart hammered, and his teeth chattered in the cold. He closed his eyes, let hope fly from his heart, and

133

waited for the end. It was what it was. Nothing he had tried had worked. Everything had gone wrong. The future was as grey and uncertain as this breath that now enveloped him.

But to his surprise, the breath did not smother or poison him. Instead, it curled and formed into a warmth on Little-Hare's other side. He didn't even need to turn or look, or cock his ear, to know who it was.

He could feel him: old, soft and grey, and see-through as a bright bubble in a fish-road. As if he had never been lost, but still lived, upright, grave and good.

His eyes full, Little-Hare turned to the ghostly figure.

Fath-hare, he said.

Fath-hare's spect-hare nodded and chewed.

This land has changed so much, my son and hare, he said. *Once this was a greensward, before it was turned over to making human food. That was what we called this place. Only it weren't just green, were it? There were all the colours, on the edge, and all around. Forget-me-nots, blue as a summer sky. White clouds of groundsel, pansies of every hue . . . and hare bell, of course.* Fath-hare let out a big sigh, as if he could see all these flowers before him in the dark.

I can't do it, Fath-hare. I've failed. The little hare's ears drooped in shame. *I was chosen and now I've let everyone down. Again. I'm sorry.*

The spect-hare rested an invisible paw upon the back of his neck.

Come, son and hare, no more of that. You have a long race yet to run. Those flowers have gone, but they could return.

How can one hare stop a Terribleness? I couldn't even save you, my own fath-hare. The great wet has destroyed so much of our valley. What if the fires come too?

The ghostly figure drifted in front of Little-Hare, his gossamer whiskers twitching. *Did I teach you nothing?*

Yes, Fath, but—

Has not a hare strong legs, swifter than any beast for furlongs around?

Yeah, but—

Has not a hare long ears, that can hear the wind before it grazes his fur?

Of course, only—

And has not a hare a cunning mind, that can outwit even . . . a buzzard?

Sometimes, I guess.

Well, then!

The spect-hare shook his head in a way that Little-Hare remembered so deeply, and longing and love for his lost fath-hare filled his being, and he wanted to rest his head against his warm fur, like when he had been but a leveret, crouching in the green.

In the dark, the spect-hare glimmered with mist. *There is one thing that might still help you stop this plague.*

The human talked about a cure.

*Aye, and any cure will need a wildflower I did not

name before. One that has grown on this island, since it was first formed. It thrives here still, despite everything. If you can but find this flower, then . . .*

Fath-hare nodded his head once more, and then began to melt away, a streak of silver slipping over the hill, into the shadows. Little-Hare half-started after him.

What's it called?

The luminous mist had nearly faded, so Little-Hare had to close his eyes so he could concentrate and hear the answer.

This flower has grown here since the beginning of things. It grows for us always, through the good times and the bad, and even though it may be harder to find right now, you have my word, it will always still be there. It can be found in the toughest of places, surviving against all the odds, because that is its nature.

Don't leave me, Fath-hare, please . . .

The voice, soft and kind, persisted.

*The worse things are, the more this flower thrives. It lights up the darkest corners, and spreads

over the stoniest ground. If you find it, and hold on tight, there will be a brighter dawn for this world, I promise.*

Only the faint outline of his fath-hare now remained, on the ridge of the hill, and what was sparkling mist and what was bright stars in the sky, it was hard to tell. But the voice was strong, and warm, and full of love.

You will find this flower, my son. For its name is hope.

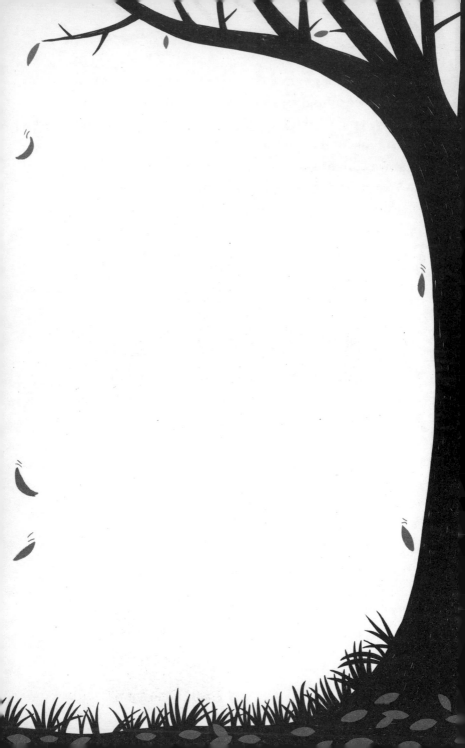

PART 3 :
A TERRIBLENESS

Little-Hare took his fath-hare's words into his hare-heart and held them there. He knew they would be a store of the greenest green for his soul to feed on, even in the toughest of times.

So, over the following nights, as the Hare Moon waned to its last quarter, Little-Hare took charge. His fath-hare had spoken truth to him. He *was* strong, swift, alert and cunning. The bull had chosen him for a reason. He *could* do this. Not just for Mooncalf but for every animal in the valley.

First, the calf had to be kept as safe as possible. With Harvest Mouse, he led her from the Wheat Between Woods into Badger Beech Copse, to keep her in the shade, out of the growing heat. This involved a tense conversation with the badgers, who spoke on behalf of the foxes, weasels and stoats that also made the copse their dwelling place. (But not the hedgehogs. The hedgehogs always spoke for themselves.)

Brock, the oldest of the badgers, stared at the Mooncalf in amazement, gazing at her gleaming silvery white skin. *She don't look ill!*

Little-Hare shook his head. *It's not like that. You can't tell by looking. The human explained. It's a slow disease, burning her up inside – over time. We've only got till the next full moon.* He glanced up uneasily at the sky.

*But why *our* dwelling, and not somewhere else?*

Because yours is the most out of the way spot, said Little-Hare. *The only place on the farm we can keep her safe, until we . . . find a cure.*

And how you goin' to do that, then?

I'm . . . looking for a flower of hope.

I ain't ever heard of no flower of hope before, littl'un. Not in our woods, that's for sure. The badger knotted his bushy eyebrows, and glanced around, lowering his voice. *What we're more worried about is other beasts thinkin' we gave 'er this dratted plague in the first place. We don't want our copse becoming a Forest of the Dead, now.*

Little-Hare shuddered at the mention of the mysterious, sacred woodlands, where many animals went to die when it was their time. He hoped his journey to one was a long time away.

Don't give me no loose talk, Harvest Mouse began to

sing, strutting along a mossy log. *Don't judge me by the way I walk.*

That won't happen, said Little-Hare hurriedly. *You have our word.*

Well, suppose we can't stop yer, said Brock, padding back off towards his sett. Then he turned around to growl at them. *An' you're sure badgers can't get it?*

Little-Hare wasn't sure at all. He was as far from sure as could be. But he had no other choice.

As far as I know! said Little-Hare as breezily as he could. *Look at me, I'm fine.* But then he added, just in case, *Perhaps keep your distance if you can, though . . .*

Brock thought for a moment, scowling.

Very well! But you'd better be right, littl'un.

He lumbered off into the leafy gloom. Little-Hare followed, leading Mooncalf to a fish-path that trickled through the middle of the copse. He stroked her soft back with his forefeet and nuzzled her while she drank.

Shall I sing you a— piped up a voice from the long reeds on the water's edge.

No! said Little-Hare, though the harvest mouse sang another one anyway.

Our world is ending, so why are we pretending . . . that it's not?

Mooncalf ate. Mooncalf drank. Mooncalf slept. She even nodded her head to the mouse's tunes (despite being warned not to by the hare). She *seemed* better.

But as the harvest mouse's songs rose and fell over the

golden opens, time marched on. And then, the moment Little-Hare had feared since the night of Bull's dream arrived.

The new Cow Moon.

It began to wax into life. Little-Hare's task was made harder still by the weather. White out of winter, a wet and a landslip were followed by unbroken blue skies and burning heat, of the kind which few animals could remember ever experiencing before.

Dandelion Hill, when it at last dried out, was now a melted mess of turf and earth. *Like a giant piece of rotten fruit,* was how Little-Hare described it to Mouse.

At the top, there was now just a huge, scorched crater of mud, rock and roots. Some animals thought this crater looked like a mouth, stuck in a perpetual scream. They called it Bull's Bellow, for the earthy jaws, frozen open for eternity, reminded them of their Wildness's bellowing call. But Bull himself would no longer be able to tell Little-Hare, or any creature, more of his dream.

He had been one of the first victims of the great wet. Chained into his concrete pen, as the water rushed in, he had roared and kicked, but no one came. The waters rose inside and out, until finally the pressure was too great, and the prison gave way, collapsing down upon his mighty head.

It was the end of Bull, their Wildness and protector for so many moons.

In normal times, the tragic death of a noble Wildness would have been all the animals talked about. There would have been mourning and remembrance. A council to elect a new Wildness, gossip about the contenders, political schemes –

But these were *not* normal times.

His was just one death of hundreds to mourn. In the face of a great wet, which had taken so many, so suddenly, such once-heavy matters suddenly seemed as light as the passing dandelion seeds, borne on the wind.

So all alone, using every moment he could, Little-Hare searched for the flower of hope his fath-hare had told him about. He combed every open, scoured under every hedge, and sniffed out the shadiest corners of every wood. But he knew the names of every flower he found already.

There were tasty leaves of sorrel to nibble at in the verges. Tall flag irises, the colour of the sun itself, stood guard over the banks of the fish-road. Creamy white honeysuckle crept up the side of the farmhouse porch.

He asked a moth one evening. *I'm looking for a flower of hope . . . it's grown here since the beginning of things?*

Does it have an irresistibly bright light?

I don't know, said Little-Hare, downcast.

Then I can't help you! said the moth, fluttering off over the long grass.

A red-legged partridge pecked briskly along the edge of the open, followed by her seven chicks, who struggled to keep up with her, not least because they kept stopping to forage for bugs and flies.

Flower of what? said the partridge. *Sorry, can't stop now! Feeding time! I'll never hear the end of it if we don't get on!*

As she stepped smartly through a gap in the hedge into the next open, followed by her brood, the little hare's ears fell flat. But he would not give up. He sniffed under the great green spread of the oak. He called out to the swallows, who told him to ask the worms, who told him to ask the bats.

But not a single other animal had ever heard of this flower, never mind seen one.

Little-Hare wondered if the human had survived the great wet, and whether he might be able to help. But when he dared approach the farm, there were too many people everywhere, repairing their own buildings, stone by stone.

He had to swerve out of the way to avoid the long tail pipe of some human contraption they had brought in, his eyes widening in amazement at this complicated human machinery that steadily sucked out the last of the water from the submerged yard.

Little-Hare retreated to a safer distance and watched as vehicles from outside drew up alongside the fish-road. To his surprise, the humans did not fish out the avalanche of rubbish that had ended up in the water after the storm, but just left it bobbing there. Instead, they constructed high walls alongside its banks.

The sun beat down day after day, and the nights were never cool. Little-Hare watched the humans rebuild their world while his grew hotter and hotter.

He had searched every last nook of the valley. He had chewed petals, sniffed leaves, pawed under rocks, even stuck his head under water in fish-paths and bogs, but no flower had he found that he didn't know the name of already.

The days grew longer and longer. The shortest night of the year, the full Cow Moon, was nearly upon them. If Little-Hare did not save Mooncalf by then, the Terribleness would come.

He hurried back to Badger Copse, lost in thought and worry. Butterflies were dancing over the wheat in the golden light as he approached the harvest mouse, perched on the end of his mossy log.

For once he was not singing.

I've searched everywhere, Mouse, Little-Hare said in desperation. *Everywhere. There is no flower of hope. At least, not in this valley . . .* He paused, puzzled.

The mouse was frozen with shock, trembling with fear.
What is it?

Something's happened. I'll show you.

Mouse sprang off into the wood. Silently, Little-Hare followed him to the fish-path, where Mooncalf lay shivering in the shade, presenting just a pale bony back to them in the dusk.

147

I don't get it, said Little-Hare. And then Mooncalf stiffly turned her head.

The hare recoiled in horror. Not because of her angular, skinny frame, the alabaster hide hanging off her in rolls as she lost more and more weight. Not because of the sheen of sweat that glistened all over her.

But because of her eyes.

In the shadow of the tall-home tops, they glowed, like burning embers of a fire, with a deep, bloody, red.

There was only one thing this could mean. Little-Hare turned to the quivering Harvest Mouse.

I think this is it, he said. *This is the Terribleness. It's begun.*

Perhaps it was Little-Hare's imagination, but the air seemed to rush colder and faster between his ears the higher he went. The ground was dark beneath his galloping paws, and the way ahead was only just lit by dim moonlight.

Faster! Faster! You . . . have . . . to run faster. He urged himself on, but it was no use.

Mooncalf had red eyes. The full Cow Moon was here, and a Terribleness was upon them. The only question now was whether Little-Hare could stop it spreading. He needed a cure.

He had already tried everywhere he could think of to look for the flower of hope. Everywhere.

Is there anything else your fath-hare told you that might be useful? the Harvest Mouse had demanded.

Little-Hare knitted his brow in thought.

He said it was a plant that has grown on this island for ever.

So has cabbage. That doesn't help us much.

And that . . . it was hard to find.

He wasn't wrong there.

But he said it would still be growing, surviving against the odds, even in the toughest of places.

And now, he was headed to exactly that: the toughest of places.

Everything that made him feel safe was behind him. The twisting roots and ferny undergrowth of Badger Beech Copse. Wheat opens that whispered softly to him as he slipped between their stalks. Even the farm, twinkling with indoor light, breathing the gentle murmur of animal life that ran through it day and night, felt safer than this.

Little-Hare headed towards a hilltop that was blasted into an eternal scream of mud and rock and roots.

Do you remember, Run-Hare, he panted to himself softly, as he padded across the barren ground, *when we used to watch the sunset from here?*

Now it was a place which no creature dared visit any more.

Bull's Bellow.

The precious Hare Circle, which he had first seen as a young leveret in terrified awe, uprooted and destroyed. Some of the stones had slid down the hill, others had fallen, and only a couple were still just standing, slanted to a dangerous degree, as if they might topple over at any moment. So the hare trod carefully as he came into the crater of the Bull's Bellow. Even in the gloom, he could sense the shadowy contours, as if his world had been stripped bare, and exposed the bone beneath.

Dandelion Hill had been scalped.

Two ancient pines had been uprooted, and the gaping holes they left were blind eye sockets above the silent scream of the scooped-out bowl of dried mud and chalk below. Little-Hare's heart sank.

Nothing could grow here. What were you thinking, you stupid hare?

Mouse was only trying to help, but what did he know? There was no flower of hope in the Bellow. There weren't even any flowers. What there was, in this bleak and featureless place, was a sense of deep despair which leached into Little-Hare's heart.

He knew being chosen as a hero would involve running fast. He could do that.

And battling adversaries, he could do that too, still feeling the tightness of the buzzard wound in his belly. He had been brave in the human cabin, hadn't he? He had survived the great wet and taken the mouse and the calf with him too.

But none of the animal stories and dreams had prepared him for this.

Loneliness.

One little animal on his own up here, every instinct told him to turn and run back to the wood – until his ears

pricked and his nose twitched. At first, he thought it was the fresh summer breeze drifting through the ring of savaged greenery that fringed the crater.

A harmless rustle.

But it wasn't.

His ears swivelled. He could hear voices. Animal voices. A low muttering, that wouldn't go away. Unable to control his instinct, he bobbed up, no longer hidden.

Hello? he said, swaying backwards and forwards, as his voice echoed around the dusty hollow.

The muttering abruptly stopped.

Little-Hare wrinkled his nose, sniffing the air. He dropped back to all fours and was about to race down the hill, when the whispering started again.

It was sharper and more urgent.

He stood up for a second time. *I can hear you!* he said, hoping he had concealed the tremors of fear in his voice. *Who is that?*

The whispering grew louder. There was the sound of scurrying feet. Little-Hare crouched down as flat to the dusty earth as he could. When he looked up again, he was encircled by pairs of eyes, bright in the night.

And slowly, the whisperers revealed themselves.

He softened.

They were nothing to be frightened of, for they were as frightened as he. They were *more* frightened. There were young quivering roe deer calves, their noses soft and wet, still ungainly on their long thin legs. Fox and badger cubs eyed each other warily, looking ready to transform at any moment into a fighting, whirling ball of fur.

The tall-homes may have been uprooted but that didn't mean they couldn't be full of life. Fledgling starlings, blackbirds and skylarks hopped about on their dark roots. There were the red-legged partridge chicks whose mother had shooed him away. Little-Hare even spied a young robin, wailing at all the others: *This is *my* dead tall-home! Now hop it, or I'll get my dad!*

In fact, now the whisperers had revealed themselves, they were no longer quiet. A tawny owlet cheeped in the darkness, and Little-Hare could just make out some bat pups swooping overhead, chasing after the many flies in the air. The farm beasts were represented by some very noisy lambs, piglets, kid goats and chicks, standing at a wary distance from the wild creatures of open and wood.

The hazy Cow Moon night was full of noise. There was life still in Dandelion Hill; there always would be.

But, from a blurry darkness beneath an overhanging jumble of roots, came a voice that rose above the others. And Little-Hare knew straight away that he was not going to find any rare wildflower here.

He had found something much, much better.

A voice that filled him with hope from the ends of his claws to the tips of his ears. The best hope of all, the hope that comes from realising you are not as alone in the world as you thought you were.

You took your time, little broth-hare.

153

Run-Hare!

And then, even though the world still was a frightening place, the two hares jumped, embraced and danced. They licked and groomed each all over, hardly able to believe that either still lived.

I thought you'd been taken by a buzzard— said Run-Hare.

I thought I'd lost you to the great wet— said Little-Hare at the same time.

Then they stopped and looked at each other and laughed. Never before had one small hare felt happier to see his bigger sibling. Suddenly, the world was not as dangerous and doomed as he thought. Little-Hare and Run-Hare were together again, and together, what could stop them? For as long as they could nuzzle close, plagues and great wets might take their course, but they would always have each other.

Then Little-Hare remembered that they had company. He stepped back from his sist-hare and looked again at the circle of eyes in the dark.

Who are your friends?

WHO DO YOU THINK? said a voice from mid-air. There was a flash of fire, and he saw the crested waxwing hovering in the air, her ringed eyes darker and her cheeks rosier than ever before.

And what do you want now? said Little-Hare.

To help you! said Run-Hare. *I knew from a dream at Hare Circle that, somehow, somewhere, you were still

alive. The bull's dream foretold
you were chosen to stop the Terribleness
and save us all. But he never said anything about
you having to do it alone.*

Little-Hare couldn't speak.

Well, COME ON, said Waxwing. *There is no time
for moping! What do you need?*

He shook himself together. *I have found the mooncalf.*

The young animals burst into a frenzy of questions:
Is she safe? *What is the Terribleness?* *Has it arrived?*
which were so many and so loud that the waxwing had
to quieten them down.

For goodness' sake, LET THE HARE SPEAK!

He paused till all was quiet again in the hollow. *She
is safe for now, out of sight in Badger Beech Copse,
protected by Harvest Mouse, Brock and his badgers . . .
but she is very ill with a plague.*

A plague? said Run-Hare, who suddenly felt cold
to her bones, despite the summer night.

*A plague which is burning her up from the inside.
Her eyes have gone red . . . I think it is the beginning
of the Terribleness. We have had the white, the
wet . . . the omens have all passed as foretold. There
is only the fire still to come. When you thought the
buzzard had taken me, I was captured by a human,
who had the mooncalf.*

Humans! I knew it! yelled
one of the piglets.

Wait, said Little-Hare. *This one was trying to help us; I really believe that. He listened to me. I can talk to him.*

You can talk to a human? Run-Hare's eyes nearly popped out of her head, and there was a commotion among the young.

How?

Does he say anything interesting?

Can you see inside his head as well? Could we talk to him?

Little-Hare waved a paw trying to calm them down.

I don't know how yet . . . it's a gift he has, to talk to all animals, not just me. He would have told me more . . . then the great wet came . . . I haven't seen him since. All I know is that my fath-hare came to me in a dream and said that our only way to save Mooncalf is to find a flower of hope and make a cure.

His audience was now silent again. Not one creature there knew of this flower, not even the waxwing, who knew most things. Little-Hare sank a little.

*But I can't find it. I have searched everywhere. *Everywhere.**

Then are we lost, broth-hare? said Run-Hare.

Never! NEVER! cried the waxwing, flaming behind her.

Waxwing is right, said Little-Hare. *I can't find this flower . . . but perhaps the humans can. They have magic . . . they have conquered this world. If anyone knows, then they will. If the human who took me survived the great wet . . . we could talk to him—*

Then . . . perhaps we should start . . . by trying to find the human who talks? said Run-Hare.

To the farmhouse! cried Waxwing.

The young wild needed no further encouragement, and they swept after the bird and the two hares down the hill. As they hurtled over the ragged rubble left by the landslide, they could just hear the distant strains of a harvest mouse, in a distant wheat open, singing the sweetest, saddest song they ever heard.

But what they didn't notice was another hare, loitering in the shadows of Bull's Bellow, the surliest of his kind. He had been watching them and smacking his lips as he did. A darkness, that was not purely from the shadows of the small hours, soured his features. He rubbed his paws with satisfaction.

Finally, after nights of waiting, Bite-Hare had what he needed.

An opportunity.

As the young animals made their way to the farm in the hazy dawn shadow of Dandelion Hill, from a distance their wings might have been banners, and their tails might have been signs. They chose to move as one down the slope, in a single formation, like geese sawing across a winter sky.

I should tell you, said Run-Hare to her broth-hare, as they leaped over the ugly mounds and ditches that now scarred their valley, *that I saw Fath-hare just as you did.*

You had a dream of him?* said Little-Hare, taken aback.

Of course! She glared at him sideways as they ran, fleet-footed as ever. *He was my fath-hare too, you know!*

Did he tell you to find a flower of hope as well?

Yes. Good old Fath-hare.

Little-Hare paused for a moment, panting. The

remaining green sparkled with more morning drops of dew than there were stars in the sky, he reckoned.

For a moment, up there in the Bull's Bellow, he said, *I thought he might have meant you. I wondered if you were the flower of hope.*

Now Run-Hare stopped too. They had run far ahead of the others, as hares always do, and sat on the new lower crest of the hill, formed out of rubble and soil dumped by the great wet as it had rushed down. Already grasses and wildflowers were sprawling through the cracks. Nature hadn't waited long; it never did.

The two hares watched as the day blossomed into life, their long black ears fringed by the flaming corncockle fire of sunrise.

Do I look like a flower to you?

In a way, that moment, in that place, after so long – she had done.

Hardly.

Well, then.

Little-Hare crumpled a little, sinking down into the earth. He was not sure how much disappointment he could bear. Run-Hare sighed, and gently placed one of her paws on top of his.

Did Fath-hare say the flower of hope would be easy to find?

No, but—

Was I easy to find?

*It took me a whole moon! I had to climb right to the

top of the hill and everything . . .* He could feel her looking at him, in that way she had since they were small. Then, it was too much, they couldn't keep up the pretence any longer, and were rolling and laughing, paws in the air.

I can't believe you thought I was the flower of hope!

*What was I thinking? *You*, a flower?*

But they could hear the other animals approaching fast behind and pulled themselves together.

*So if you're *not* the flower of hope . . .* Little-Hare said, scratching the soil off his fur with his paws.

Then we keep looking until we find it, don't we? said Run-Hare. She was already sailing off down the slope, towards the farm fence. *And don't stop looking until you do!*

As the animals approached their destination, they grew in number, as word spread that the hares were finally going to save Mooncalf and stop the Terribleness. Some of the older animals that had survived the great wet grudgingly joined in, including Ram and Ewe.

As sheep, we don't like to make a habit of following what others do, but just on this occasion, I suppose we'll make an exception! Ewe had said huffily, as her lambs implored her to join their gathering.

Robin had somehow found his way to the front of the crowd and danced from animal head to animal head. *This is my protest!* he sang loudly as the sun rose and rose. *You lot, back off! I'm at the front.*

160

His fledgling chirruped back. *No, *you* back off! I was here first. *Dad.**

Pretty Pony called from her paddock, *I wish I knew how to make a placard. But it's difficult with these hooves.* None of the others knew what a placard was. They only knew that they wanted the humans to listen to them, before it was too late.

By the time the farmer stirred from his bed that morning, the barn roofs of Old Farm were covered in young birds, from sombre crow chicks to squeaking pigeon squabs. A clattering of young jackdaws strutted cockily by the chimney stacks of the farmhouse itself, crying out, which in the animal tongue sounded like, *All right, Jack?* but nobody ever discovered who Jack was. Chiffchaffs tweeted back to them from the farmer's garden, and a clutch of stock doves sung sweetly from their barn nests.

Swallows and swifts looped after flies in the velvet sky above. Butterflies hung in rippling, living curtains over every fence and wall. Bees flocked against outbuilding windows in swarms, blocking out the light.

On the ground, the young animals filled every space that could be filled. The piglets stood in front of the tool shed, the lambs blocked the entrance to the garage, and the kid goats encircled the entire farmhouse. Fox and badger cubs patrolled the drive, while adders and freshly arrived grass snakes draped themselves over the entrance gates just in case anyone thought they could walk away.

The animals of Dandelion Hill were on strike. (Apart from the hedgehoglets, who had been summoned home for feeding, but had sent supportive messages via the wasps.)

Now, fully assembled, they fell quiet.

They stood, lay, crouched or hovered in near silence. At the front of them all stood Little-Hare and Run-Hare, proud of their night's work. Waxwing, who hovered triumphantly over their heads, had been right. It was easier to organise working together, and that was how they had persuaded so many of the animals to join their march on the farmhouse – a cry for help from all the voices of the valley.

That has been the easy part, thought Little-Hare.

The human dwelling stood before them, stark and silent against the wakening sky, as the lowly beasts of the wild grimaced in its shadow. Little-Hare could hear every animal behind him: the weight of their breath, the flutter of their hearts, the flap of a wing or the scratch of a claw.

He and his sist-hare had led them here.

Are you sure this will work? whispered Run-Hare to her broth-hare.

What else can we do? There's no way you or I can stop the Terribleness burning Mooncalf up on our own. Professor Jaynes said he had tests and all sorts. He must have survived the great wet. Humans can survive anything!

And if you're wrong?

Little-Hare was saved from answering by patches of light that began to appear in the human dwelling. Figures inside moved around in silhouette, though Little-Hare couldn't tell if the professor was among them. The dogs inside kicked off with barks and growls.

One of the humans would come outside any minute, he was sure. They had to.

WHAT are you waiting for? urged Waxwing.

Yes, go on, said Run-Hare, a gentle paw on his back. *This was your idea, after all.*

Little-Hare nodded. But in his belly, he still felt the tightness of the wound from when he last visited the farm, and the buzzard had nearly taken him. He glanced anxiously up at the sky. And in his heart, he still didn't know if he could fully trust the human who had stuck metal twigs and transparent worms into his haunch. Not to mention that the scent of the dogs from the dwelling was so overpowering he felt sick to his guts.

If Dog came out rather than a human, then it was all over.

Go on, murmured Run-Hare. *A hare cannot watch all the time. Sometimes we need to act.*

She was right. If he had only acted in the wheat open last summer.

Keeping low to the ground, Little-Hare crept out into the open near the farmhouse. He loped up to the large wooden door, cracked and peeling, and as he had once seen humans do, rapped a clawed paw against the wood.

There was a faint echo inside. But nothing else happened. So he tapped again.

And again, drawing his claws down against the door for good measure. No one came.

He looked around him in puzzlement. Run-Hare joined him, knocking with her paws and dragging her claws down the wooden panels.

And still no one answered.

Other animals stepped forward now, encouraged and intrigued. The two hares made way for lambs and kid goats to butt the door, making it shudder. From inside, they could hear the dogs barking the walls down, but no one even went near the door.

Mystified, the birds watching from the roof tops flew down to the windows and perched on the upper floor sills. They pecked at the glass and flapped their wings.

Could the humans inside not see the animals?

Make more noise! urged Little-Hare. *Then they'll have to come!*

The young animals had lost their fear now, and began bleating, chirruping and bellowing as loudly as they could.

In return, they could hear human noises from within. A murmur of conversation, clinking dishes, the hum of a radio.

Still not one human answered the animals.

This isn't right, said Little-Hare, and he darted around the sides of the building, trying to find another way in. Every door was locked, every window sealed firmly shut. Yet he knew the farmer and his family were inside. He could see the man-made light, the dim blur of their figures, and hear their chatter.

He sprinted back round to the front, where the animals he had led all the way here were now gathered round the building. They were only young and did not have the full size and strength of their elders, but they pushed against that door as if their lives depended on it.

The morning had arrived, and the sun was blazing.

What were they playing at?

Little-Hare leaped on to the backs of some pigs so he could see into the front room window. Even though he knew the humans inside could not understand, he roared through the glass.

Mooncalf has red eyes. Soon she will be burned up completely, and the Terribleness will spread to us all. Much of our home has been destroyed, we have lost so many we love – please, listen to us, we need your help!

All the young animals from the valley gathered around the house joined him, their voices raised in desperation and anger. They called for help till they had no breath left in their lungs. But the humans never came out. Was it because they did not hear the cries, or because they were frightened, or because they chose to ignore them? Nobody could say for sure.

165

Only one thing was certain.

As the creatures outside peered at those within, looking from blank face to blank face – if they had once been their fellow animals, it was no longer possible to tell.

I just don't understand, said Little-Hare for about the fifteenth time to his sist-hare, as they headed back up the hill. *Why didn't they come out? There were so many of us, we couldn't have made more noise. They *must* have known we were there.*

I told you. They don't care. They were ignoring us. It doesn't matter how many of us there were, or how much noise we made. The humans don't care about any Terribleness. We are on our own.

But Professor Jaynes—

Either wasn't there, or doesn't care any more either.

So what do we do now? said Little-Hare, as they approached the welcoming tall-homes of Badger Beech Copse.

Just as I said before, we keep looking, said Run-Hare, but she sounded less convinced this time.

And if we're too late, and the Terribleness spreads?

I don't know! Aren't you meant be the chosen one? Think of something!

Little-Hare stopped and stared at his sist-hare with his glassy eyes. *That doesn't make it easy, you know! This is the hardest thing I've ever . . . since we lost Moth-hare and Fath-hare. I will put it right. Put it *all* right. But you've got to trust me.*

He bounded off ahead of her in a fury.

It wasn't your fault, you know! she called after him, but he didn't reply.

Bite-Hare squatted low in the Wheat Between the Woods as the two other hares returned. He peered through the stalks; the tips of his ears just visible above them. They were so lost in conversation, they had no idea they were being spied on.

He saw one race ahead and the other slide after him into the dappled shade of Badger Beech Copse and clenched his lips tight in satisfaction. He had watched their failure of a protest unfold at Old Farm from a safe distance. These hares were so weak, he thought. They believed they could persuade humans to help them, when any animal with a brain in their skull could have seen that would never work.

Now he would show them the error of their ways. All of them.

Looking around to make sure he was unobserved, he sliced hard at his own nose, so blood trickled down his face. He scratched some more, pulling at his ears till fur came free in tufts. Then he rolled around in the soil between the wheat, over and over, until he was completely filthy.

Then, a strange light in his eyes, he slunk towards the deepening shadows of the beech wood.

Little-Hare was hunched over the small fish-path that ran through Badger Beech Copse, a bunch of dock leaves in his mouth. He dunked them in the cool water that tinkled over gravel and moss-covered rocks, and darted back, the leaves ice cold and dripping wet, to soothe Mooncalf. Run-Hare also comforted the calf with kind words and the harvest mouse softly hummed lullabies, for what else could they do?

But Mooncalf grew weaker with every passing moment.

Her eyes burned the deep shining red of rowan berries, and the hotter they burned, the thinner she seemed to grow. Little-Hare was sure there was less of her than there had been the night before. It was as if she was fading into thin air, in danger of disappearing completely.

The evening light filtered down through the beech canopy, and what should have been another long golden summer night shimmered into being. The wood felt very

quiet and very still for a moment,
and the calf's carers watched the evening
sun dancing through the leaves, lost in their own
thoughts.

Did the human tell you how, sang the mouse, *he plans to save our cow?*

The hares shook their heads and then a rustling in the ferns behind put them on their guard. There was a whimpering sound coming from a clump of bracken.

Go away, hissed Run-Hare. *Whoever you are. This is a place of plague.*

The whimpering just grew louder, interspersed with a wailing cough.

Little-Hare took a step towards the coughing clump. He had seen off a buzzard, survived the human cabin and a great wet. He had dared to explore Bull's Bellow and found Run-Hare. He had even scratched at the human dwelling! Something whimpering and coughing behind ferns did not scare him.

He cautiously parted the springy coils with a paw and took a step straight back.

Bite-Hare! What happened?

The larger hare opened his mouth, revealing his bloodied gums. His face was a mess, his body covered in scratches and mud. *Dog and his mutt gang,* he said weakly. *I just outran them, but they had a go before I did.*

Run-Hare leaped to his side. *You were

there at the farm? With us? I
was so worried . . . after you left me the
way you did.*

A bubble of blood appeared at Bite-Hare's lips.
*Forget about all that. I was trying to find the human
for you. His magic. Everyone was saying that he could
talk to hares, I thought I could—*

He coughed for some time, his body rattling.

Don't just stand there! snapped Run-Hare to her
dumbfounded broth-hare. *More dock leaves, quick!*

Slowly, Bite-Hare recovered himself, breath by
breath. *I found him . . . in a yard. When you were
all . . . by the house.*

He's alive! Does he have the cure?

*I . . . don't know. He wouldn't tell me. Then the
dogs . . .*

He started to splutter again, worrying if he was
overdoing it, but Run-Hare just laid a paw on his
brow. *There, there,* she said. *You're safe now,
take your time.*

Little-Hare returned with more dock leaves, and
they mopped Bite-Hare up.

It's not so bad after all, is it? said Run-Hare.

Bite-Hare fluttered his eyes, and still acted as
weak as he could manage. *I don't feel so good
inside . . . Dog charged at me . . .* He coughed
some more. *But the man gave me a
message. For Little-Hare.*

For me?

You alone. The man wants you to meet him tonight . . . in the yard.

Bite-Hare screwed up his mouth, quivered his whiskers, and forced his whole healthy body to vibrate with pain. *He . . . has something to give you.*

*

As darkness fell that evening, Little-Hare ran past the side of a barn damaged in the great wet, its holes covered with sheets of plastic that flapped ominously in the wind. He ducked under a scaffolding tower parked alongside it, hopping over tubs of mortar, rubble sacks and toolboxes. The farmyard felt dark and quiet; the young protestors had not returned.

He emerged from the scaffolding to find himself in a small yard, with dark ways off between the four barns which surrounded it. This was where Bite-Hare had sent him, but there was a strange smell about the place, which made Little-Hare pause. He sniffed the concrete ground, which, by the dim light of the farm's security night lamps, looked stained with something.

Professor? he said to the empty square. Perhaps he was early.

Little-Hare sniffed some more. He saw the moonlight glint off the hooks and racks hanging in the barns on either side, the saws and knives neatly arranged on tables. Rubber hoses were coiled tight in dark corners like sleeping snakes. But they had not washed all the blood of the farm beasts slaughtered here away. It stained the ground in black sprays and blots, all that now remained of so many that once walked the green opens of this wild.

But it was not dead animals he could smell. Something else.

Professor? Is that you? Where are you?

He shook his head to rid himself of the unpleasant images, and loped towards the nearest alley, but froze long before he got there.

For now, too late, he recognised the scent –

The smell he feared the most. A scent of betrayal.

How could he have been so stupid? He had been blinded by his desperation to find a cure quickly. The chosen one? Chosen idiot, more like. Now he was alone in the farmyard, with the animals he feared the most on earth.

The toothless hare was not wrong, growled a voice from the shadows. *You must have a tiny hare-brain if you fell for his trap, you hapless hedge-squatter.*

It was Dog, edging forward out of the dark – tail up, crouched low – his head a block of teeth and scars in the moonlit yard.

Little-Hare tried to run, but Lurcher sprang into the hare's path, snarling.

Yeah, you pathetic pintail! We've got you now!

Little Hare pelted across the yard to another alleyway, where Hound stood on his huge paws, slobbering and panting in anticipation of a good kill.

Me hungry, said Hound simply.

Little-Hare was trapped.

Wait! he said, as the pack closed in. *I'm here to help all of us. Mooncalf is fading, the Terribleness is here. You're meant to be Guardians!*

Dog threw back his misshapen head and laughed heartily at the moon. Then a vicious snarl ripped across his face.

A Guardian of the farm, not you. Besides, do you think I care what an old dead bull said?

Even if it means we might all die? That our young ones don't have a future?

Little-Hare could not believe he was standing up to Dog. Though for once, he knew this was bigger than dogs and hares fighting and running as usual. Nothing would ever be usual again. Dog was contemptuous.

The fewer rabbits, hares and foxes I have to chase the better. All the more time for sleeping and eating. We dogs will be all right, sleeping warm in our master's house. And besides, that soft human staying with us is working on a cure. He doesn't need help from a sly still-sitter like you.

Time seemed to rebound, deadening the growls of the dogs to a distant rumble, melting the hard corners of the farmyard into a disorientating blur. Little-Hare shook himself together.

*Professor Jaynes? He's alive? Then I need to take him

to Mooncalf, immediately—*

I couldn't give a flying slipper what you need, said Dog. *Dogs only care about following orders. And my orders are to keep crop-thieving vermin out of the farm.*

With that he lowered himself into his stalking crouch, ready to leap –

Little-Hare danced aside –

Dog flew over his head, landing with a snarl on the hard stone, and roared after him.

There was no way out, but Little-Hare looked for one all the same. The lurcher was snapping, and the hound gave a throaty cry of war. He had to try and hold his nerve.

Dog was upon him again –

Little-Hare cried in alarm, and tried to scrabble up a plastic oil drum, but the sides were too smooth. He had to escape, he had to find the professor, he had to – but he slipped down, falling on to Dog, and rolled off, skidding over the concrete. Paws fell upon his back, drubbing and ripping his fur, and he somehow slithered free –

Now Lurcher bolted after him, followed by the panting hound and Dog, backing him into a corner in the slaughter barn. Dog's teeth flashed in the dark.

Little-Hare's heart hammered with terror as he searched in vain for any chink of freedom. He pawed frantically at wooden boards that did not move and could hear himself whining in fear. He tore at sacking which only flopped over his head, temporarily blinding him. Scraping away patches of dirt, he found only pitiless stone underneath.

There was nothing else for it.

He crouched deathly still, his great eyes glazed with fear, every hair on his body trembling, as he imagined the awful pain and destruction to come.

This was nature's way. Now he must accept. Chosen or not –

Little-Hare's dream was over.

Run-Hare was cleaning Bite-Hare with a tenderness that she had never expected to feel. She had been wrong about him, she thought, as she picked dirt out of his sun-flecked fur with her claws. Down in the waterlogged farm, for a moment, she thought he had lost his mind – as well as his two front teeth – but perhaps it had been shock.

Shock could do strange things to animals.

Bite-Hare had temporarily lost his mind when the great wet swept away half of Dandelion Hill. All that ranting about revenge. Who could blame him? And her poor broth-hare, after their tragedy last summer, had blanked the events from his memory. She closed her eyes for a moment. If only she could forget. The dogs, shrieking with death, as they fell upon her fath-hare and moth-hare—

No. Such thoughts were not helpful.

What Little-Hare couldn't remember wouldn't hurt him, Run-Hare had long ago decided. He would always stay well clear of the farm's ferocious protectors, he had that much sense at least.

My lady, murmured Bite-Hare as she licked some dried blood away from his ear. *You are too kind.*

And you are too brave! said Run-Hare. *To risk so much by finding the human we need.*

She rubbed a dock leaf against a nasty scratch on his nose.

How funny it was that events could change not just the world, but how you saw other creatures, she thought. Bite-Hare had been creepy and a self-obsessed show-off. A jack-hare she could have boxed for an eternal spring, rather than mate.

Run-Hare had feared the great wet had sent him insane. Her ill-timed laughter, not meant cruelly or unkindly, seemed to have tipped him over the edge.

But he had come good in the end, fighting for his wild. He had risked his life for them. It was no longer possible to hate him. And – strangest of all – as she cleaned the last of the mud from his fur, his grinding teeth replaced by a gap-toothed, lopsided expression, she was beginning to feel another emotion entirely.

You know, Bite-Hare— she started to say.

She was interrupted by the most solemn harvest mouse she had ever seen, tapping at her feet, his dark eyes bright with alarm.

178

Please! he implored. *You have to come to Mooncalf. Now! She's . . . changing.*

Little-Hare waited for oblivion. But none came. Instead, flashes of colour flew across the fuzz of his inner mind, like pheasants flapping home at dusk. His sister's amber eyes. Fath-hare's cloud-grey muzzle. The impossible silvery whiteness of Mooncalf.

His dream could not be over, because then it was over for all the others too.

Then he was back, facing a blur of yellowing teeth and a wide pink mouth. He bobbed on to his back legs, and, using his front paws, did what a hare can do.

He boxed.

What do you think you're doing, you gormless grass biter? said Dog, taken aback by the blows.

Yeah, you dopey dew hopper! sneered Lurcher, swerving each swipe.

Little-Hare paused for breath, his paws still raised.

My name is Little-Hare, he said, underlying each word with a feint, *of Dandelion Hill, and I have been chosen to save my wild from the Terribleness.*

He jabbed. He swerved. He undercut. The dogs howled and darted around him, but the more they did, the more he danced. In his mind's eye, he recalled his sist-hare on spring evenings, in happier times, and how she moved with the grace of the wind. Outstretched paws became branches of willow to duck under, their rough claws mere brambles, as he side-stepped each blow, again and again.

Around and around he spun, a whirling tornado of fur –

Yet despite his courage, there were still three dogs who wanted only his blood, and they would not stop either. So the second they drew back, tongues lolling, their sides flecked with bubbles of sweat and blood, Little-Hare did the other thing hares can do.

He ran.

In a single explosive leap, he was free of the blood-soaked slaughterhouse, skittering across the stone in the shiny dark. Little-Hare had no idea where he was going, scents attacking him from all directions: cow, sheep, feed and oil blended in one heady musk.

But he knew what he was looking for, determined to root him out this time. A human working on a magic cure.

The dogs' howls rang in his ears. He shot under the shadow of some giant human machine, all iron bumps stinking of smoke and straw stuck in mud underneath, then shot out again –

They were still behind him; he could feel their hot breath on his heels –

Hear their snouts, snuffling so eagerly for his scent –

He plunged into a water trough, soaked through, and out again!

He leaped over a freshly dug ditch, gleaming with exposed red pipe, like an artery –

Little-Hare turned, turned and turned again, but still they came. The pack of dogs chased him up a rotting old beam, and they chased him down a rippled iron roof on the other side, covering a chicken coop, the birds inside clucking wildly with alarm at the riotous clatter of paws over their heads.

He tripped off the coop into some tractor tyres that had been rolled against a wall, which wobbled over behind him with a flume of dust, and he heard the hound yelp in pain. Little-Hare jumped over an old plough and headed down a roughly surfaced track between two great barns.

There were just two dogs on his tail now, but two was enough. The track between the barns reached a dead end: a tall wall, topped with fur-tearing wire. So he dived into the barn with an open door. A wooden dwelling, with high sides but moonlight and air washing in through square holes cut out of the roof and walls.

This was not a beast dwelling; it was too spacious and airy for that.

He knew what it was.

The smell of grain was so intense, he wanted nothing more than to stop and nibble at the dusty feed. In another life, this was all his hare-dreams come at once.

A food store, one huge pile of grain, rising up to the top corners of the building. He ran up the man-made hill and it was like trying to run in the powdery white at winter, but he ran all the same, as light-pawed as he could.

Then, suddenly, he had to bring himself up short.

The grain mountain levelled out at the top. A cool night breeze came in through an opening, keeping the stored wheat dry and aired. Little-Hare sniffed the square of summer night, looked, and listened . . .

But the drop was sheer and steep. He had chosen the tallest barn in the farm, and the other roof tops spread out beneath him in the moonlit night, like shining black rocks exposed in a shallow fish-path. Directly below was the human house, all aglow with warm magic light, humming with a gentle buzz of inner life.

The professor. He was so close. He could feel him. Little-Hare snapped his head back at the two dogs triumphantly circling the bottom of the dusty hill below. Could he run past both of them?

Dog was laughing, throaty and cracked. *We've got you now, you nincompoop of a nibbler!*

Yeah, you craven creeper! added Lurcher.

Come and get me, then! said Little-Hare. He was surprised at the clearness of his own voice in the grain store; he could almost see his words twisting in the columns of dust that spiralled up from the harvested crop. Why had he said that?

He was trapped.

The mouse led the two hares deep into the beech wood, where the light filtered down through the delicate leaves and threw gentle shafts of gold over the smooth grey trunks. These elegant pillars formed a kind of avenue, which led to the fish-path, the source of Mooncalf's main relief during the summer heat. The water ran over mossy rocks and gravel and made a pealing music all of its own.

Bite-Hare see-sawed ahead of the others, leaping over the leaf-layered ground. He could dimly see the pale shape of the mooncalf up ahead. She really did seem to glow in the light. Every hair on his back fizzed with glee. His head was giddy with victory, and he licked his toothless gums with anticipation. Soon this unwelcome calf, the cause of so much grief and stress would be gone – like many, many calves before her – and life would carry on as before.

There would be no Terribleness.

That was just a story made up to scare little ones by Wildnesses. Bite-Hare would not be so easily fooled by dreams and predictions.

More importantly, once his beloved Run-Hare had recovered from the shock of losing both Little-Hare and the mooncalf . . . she would be his, no question. After all, who else would she have left? It was a kind of happy revenge, he told himself, where everyone got what they wanted. If nothing else, he had proven he could twist the worst of situations to his own ends.

What were two front teeth compared to all that?

Maybe, one day, he might even make a good Wildness . . .

But all those ideas fled his head quicker than a shock of starlings sweeping into the air when he reached the fish-path. He skidded to a halt, not able to speak at what he saw.

What is it? said Run-Hare, fast on his heels.

Then she was rendered speechless too.

The mouse clutched his paws in anxiety and fear. *For the first time in my life,* he said, *I can't think of a song. I've never seen anything like it.*

For there, right in front of their eyes, under the light of a midsummer moon, the silvery miracle that was Mooncalf was disappearing.

She wasn't just growing thinner, or weaker, or more ill (although she was all those things) – *she was beginning to vanish all together*. Her red eyes blazed fiercer than ever, as if they were the hot coals powering her transformation. But inch by inch, from her hooves to her ears, the tip of her tail to her snout, the beautiful, frost-coloured expanse of her skin was fading into air.

It was impossible. Such a thing had never been known in the valley, or in the world beyond, as far as the animals knew. But yet, it was happening. Where her skin had once sparkled like ice, now the green gleamed, and the fish-path ran full to overflowing. Where her eyes had once glowed, the stars shone bright to bursting. The mooncalf never complained, or cried out in pain, but the sadness, the regret in her eyes –

Bite-Hare stretched out a paw –

It was like trying to catch marsh breath or hitch a ride on a cloud.

She was the most beautiful animal he had ever seen. And now she was vanishing right in front of him.

My love! he cried out, prostrate on the ground. He turned on Run-Hare, in gibbering fury. *You deceiver! Why did you never tell me? This is the most beautiful thing on earth, not you!*

We tried! said Run-Hare. *But you didn't listen.*

I sang the song, but you never came along, crooned Mouse softly.

But, but . . . she's so miraculous! Magical! And now . . . she's leaving us! he wailed, and thumped the ground with his paws.

I know, said Run-Hare. *You were too late. We all were.*

So they bowed their heads, and prayed to their eternal mother, the moon, but it made no difference. Mooncalf, a miracle, born into ice and frost – was melting away.

And if that could happen, who knew what would follow?

Little-Hare edged back against the square of open barn, feeling the fresh air of the night cool upon his fur. Dog scrambled up the sandy drift of the grain mountain towards him. Lurcher tried to follow, and kept stumbling, then slipping, on her thin legs. The more she slipped, the more enraged she grew, until eventually she slithered back to the concrete floor.

Yeah, I'll keep guard here. You're dead now, though, ditch-ditherer! she snapped.

Perhaps Lurcher was right. For Dog was on him, and this time there was no escape. Little-Hare couldn't bob and box on these shifting grains. Instead, he cowered right up against the open night air. A life-threatening drop to farmhouse roof and gutter awaited if he was lucky – the solid stone of the yard far below, if he wasn't.

Dog snapped his jaws, his milky grey eyes alight with rage.

You put up more of a fight than your fath-hare and moth-hare, I'll give you that, you feeble fern-flopper. He wiped his cracked lips with a horrifically long tongue. *But I hope you taste better. They were foul. Like the vermin they were.*

He paused, tense, perhaps expecting Little-Hare to lash out, or make a last-chance dash for it. Little-Hare did neither of those things. For behind him, he sensed the moon, mother of miracles, his constant guide and saviour. As her light shone through the grain store opening, in the silver glow, he saw the shadowy traces of those who had fallen before him.

The ghostly spirits of the hunted hare at his back, the legions of his kind felled on the wide opens of this island since dawn first broke. He had been chosen by the dream to keep the wild safe. Not just this wild, but every animal in the world. Now it was time to break the spell. The hares in the moon were watching. Moth-hare and Fath-hare too, he just knew. It was time to make them proud.

He stopped cowering. He did what dogs hate, and looked him direct in the eye.

Dog, he said, and he was the first ever hare to say this, *I am no longer afraid. Not of you, not of the Terribleness, no, not even of death. Our life is too short and too precious to spend it living in fear.*

And he turned and sprang out of
the window, into the eternal light of the moon.

He rolled in the air, limbs flailing –

Falling and falling, his heart plunging –

A hideous scrabbling, shrieking, hot-breathed mass of dog leaped through the air behind him, casting a shadow over the farmhouse roof –

They both slammed into the pitched tiles, cracking several, leaving themselves winded but alive. Little-Hare clung to the ridge of the roof with his claws, backing away from Dog, who had a line of dark blood trickling out of his nose.

The hare's hunter was bruised but triumphant, hobbling towards him, claws also clamped to the tiled spine of the house.

Don't mind me, I love the taste of blood. Mine's all right, but compared to yours . . .

Little-Hare was right at the end of the roof. There was no way off other than to the ground, a fall neither of them would survive. But just because Little-Hare was no longer afraid, that didn't mean he had turned stupid. Ever since he had entered the grain store, his long ears had been scooping and channelling sound, all the noises of the farm, the land, the woods and the sky.

He had chosen his moment well. At least, he hoped he had, as he backed into a crooked smokestack, with nowhere left to run. All he could see was the glint in Dog's eye, as he sprang towards him, jaws outstretched –

Little-Hare screamed, scratching and pushing, as the heavy beast fell upon him, sinking his teeth into his fur.

And then Dog was yanked back, a look of complete surprise on his face, as he flew up into the air – hooked on a buzzard's talons.

What the—

Hey, hare! called the bird to Little-Hare, as she swung unsteadily into the air with her outsized prey. *I thought about what you said the other day. It pains me, but you're right, which is not bad for a piece of food. We do need to work together. Now scram!*

Blood ran down Little-Hare's neck, but he didn't care.

In the distance, he heard the dog roaring, *What are you going to do to me?*

The bird's reply was muffled, but it almost sounded like, *Enjoy the best meal I've had this year . . .*

And then they were gone, his two adversaries, disappearing into the darkness. Unfortunately, so was Little-Hare. Drenched in blood and sweat, he slipped and lost his balance on the roof. Lashing his claws out in vain at the tiles, he slid down them faster than a muddy bank –

His hind legs went over the edge, his tail bobbing –

His forepaws slipped off the roof, clamping on to the rickety gutter –

He hung there, swinging, gazing up at the moon in desperation. Only she could save him now.

Then he glanced through the glass in front of him.

189

At the startled human, lying on a bed, surrounded by piles of paper, and glass jars and tubes, staring back at him –

Professor Jaynes.

The man was attending to the hare's wounds again, only this time the hare was awake. And talking.

Why didn't you come out when we called from the door? We made all the noise in the world, hundreds of animals! You lot just . . . ignored us. Like we were nothing. And we're not. We've got the right to live here too, you know.

You're lucky . . . these cuts and scratches are only . . . replied Professor Jaynes, not finishing his sentence again.

He had his gloves on once more and had wiped most of the blood off with small wet white squares that stung. Now he was dabbing at the more tender cuts around Little-Hare's nose, and beneath his eyes, the delicate skin around his joints and under his belly. It all required concentration, so Little-Hare did not repeat his question, but focused on deep breathing, while the professor was absorbed in his work.

After what felt like many moons to the hare, the man stood back, peeling off his gloves, and tossing the bloodied white squares into an overflowing bucket. Then he rubbed the bridge of his nose.

Professor Jaynes looked tired. Not to mention covered in as many scratches and cuts as the hare, and bruises too.

He walked with a slight limp. The great wet had left no one unscathed. Now he hobbled over to the bed and sat down with a sigh, scattering the piles of paper on it, which fluttered into the air and fell like leaves.

I wondered what that was all about, he said. *The farmer wouldn't let any of us out. He said you were all seeking attention, and that the best thing to do when an animal does that, is to ignore them until they stop, and . . .*

But you knew better! exploded Little-Hare. *You heard us! You understand us! Why didn't you say something?*

The Professor sighed.

I'm sorry, Hare. The truth is, I was too busy up here, trying to find a way to make your calf better.

He gestured round the room and Little-Hare followed his gaze. A screen of human magic and light, like the ones in the cabin, flickered with symbols. There were vials, human scratching implements, and so much paper, covered in mystifying marks, everywhere.

Little-Hare was in awe. He knew the human magic would never be as powerful as the pull of the moon that shone on them both, but it was impressive, nevertheless. He felt his heart rise, and for a moment, didn't want to ask the question in case he was given the wrong answer. And then he remembered: he wasn't afraid any more. He *had* to ask.

Have you found a cure?

Professor Jaynes folded his arms and slumped back on the bed, watching the hare for a while. He rubbed his chin, and hummed, as if he was the one now frightened to speak. But at last, he did. *Well . . . we do now know much more than we did . . . and it's all . . . thanks to you.*

To me?

If you hadn't . . . that night . . . you know, found the calf . . . woken her out of the snow . . .

Then what?

She would already be dead. We would have been too late . . . the world would not have had advance warning of one of the most . . . deadly diseases ever.

Little-Hare was confused. *But if she had died, and I hadn't woken her, hadn't been chosen, then—*

Oh, the disease would still be here, just waiting to show itself at another time, in another beast. Only we might not know about it. We might be already experiencing a catastrophe of . . . monumental proportions. He smiled. *Your curiosity, your kindness – not to mention your bravery in looking for her in my cabin – meant I could study both of you for signs of infection. I have sent details of the disease to Facto. They will take action, trust me. You have already saved countless lives, Little-Hare, by thinking about others.*

I have? Little-Hare had never thought of himself as a creature who could save lives before. *So now you will save Mooncalf?*

Professor Jaynes leaped to his feet. With his back to the hare, he dragged a large bag out from under the bed and began stuffing it with all the different woollen skins humans liked to wear, cramming all the papers on top. *Time may be running out for Mooncalf, I'm afraid. There is only so much I can do here, and now I have to go back to my own city, where I live . . . because I've had some bad news.*

He stopped, hands on the case, unable to speak for a moment. Little-Hare wanted to pound him with his paws.

I can't imagine any worse news than there not being a cure for the calf. You promised!

My wife, Laura, said Professor Jaynes, only just able to pronounce the words. *I heard today. She is very ill herself . . . has been for some time. It was under control, but now . . . My boy, Kester. They both need me.* He turned to face the hare again, his eyes wet. *I have to go home, I'm sorry. Family first.*

Little-Hare's head swam. The papers with their scribbles, the flickering screen, seemed to fly around the room in his head. Family first. Humans first, more like. What good was any of it?

But my wild! The Terribleness!

I'm sorry, Little-Hare. I will work on the cure; you have my word. We are so close.

What am I meant to do? Then he remembered. *The flower of hope? Is that what you need to finish the cure? I will keep looking for it, we all will—*

Professor Jaynes frowned in puzzlement. *The flower of what?* He was lost in thought for a moment, before he nodded, understanding at last.

The flower of hope, he said, *is exactly what you must keep looking for, Little-Hare. You have bought us all precious time. But what began on that snowy night will change our world for ever, and was always going to – mine and yours. That doesn't mean that we can't prepare for it, that doesn't mean we can't survive, and perhaps, even . . . make what comes after a better place for us all. Humans and animals.*

Then, I've failed.

The professor exploded. It was a kind of joyful rage. *Failed? You've only just begun!*

So what must I do?

Keep looking for that flower. No matter what happens, keep looking far and wide, Little-Hare. The red-eye virus is coming. But one day – you have my word – so is hope.

So, Little-Hare did keep looking.

But if Fath's flower had been hard to find before, it grew harder still. For everything happened as the bull had predicted. What some animals had dismissed as just a dream and many had just ignored, came to pass.

The Terribleness began.

Gentle Mooncalf had faded fully into the Great Beyond, and her passing had been as quiet and modest as her life. By the time Little-Hare returned to the Badger Beech Copse, the harvest mouse greeted him with a catch in his voice.

At the end of the day, he lamented, *it was as if she just melted away.*

But Little-Hare nodded. He already knew.

He told Run-Hare everything that had happened on the farm, how Bite-Hare had sent him into a trap, and the conversation with Professor Jaynes. For a moment, his heart was full of rage, and when he saw the other hare, padding round and round in circles in the copse near Mooncalf's fish-path, he wanted to leap upon him, and tear him, and knock out his other teeth – but Run-Hare saw the look in his eyes, and stayed him softly with a paw.

I know, broth-hare, she said. *But there's no need. Look.*

Bite-Hare appeared even stranger than before. He walked around and around in circles on the same spot, a faraway, blank look in his eyes. Every now and then he would swipe the air, as if after a fly, or something only he could see.

Mooncalf! he said. *My beautiful! I will find you!*

The other two watched him for a moment, chasing invisible ghosts that only he saw, and then prepared themselves for what happened next.

For as Mooncalf had faded away, melting into the earth, the same sickness which had burned inside her was unleashed on the valley, just as the bull had warned.

As summer faded, so the damp air of autumn spread the plague faster than the leaves fell off the branches. Whatever Mooncalf had incubated inside her had grown in strength and speed, destroying as it bloomed. One evening Little-Hare watched an owl swoop down for her daily hunt, but she never returned, lying spreadeagled where she fell.

It was just the beginning.

The wild's many visitors – reed warblers, swallows

and swifts among them – bade
farewell to him from the tops of tall-
homes, as they set off on their long journeys back.
But many of them never made it past the edge of
the valley, and fell from the sky to return to the soft
earth of Dandelion Hill.

Just going for a nap, Little-Hare, said Brock the
badger, as he padded into his sett. He never re-emerged,
curled up under the ground of the beech copse with
all the other badgers, buried nose to tail.

Little-Hare sniffed at the drifts of beech nuts
carpeting the leaf-strewn earth. If only the squirrels
who should have been devouring them didn't lie
motionless alongside. The jays no longer screeched in
the tall-home tops above, and the magpie's chatter fell
silent.

Red admiral butterflies descended over piles of
fallen apples in the farm orchard, where they
remained, till a sharp wind blew them into dust.
Beehives, emptied of their queen and swarm, became
ghostly, echoing palaces.

He ran down to the fish-road for water and fresh
air, but trout, carp and pike floated to the surface, silver
bellies up, caught by the fading light of the shortening
days. A kingfisher shot by in a flash of fire, then
vanished for ever, with a distant splash.

For a while, only Robin kept
him company, still singing

every day from the solitary fence post he had chosen to isolate himself on. *No plague is going to get me! Just come and try it!*

It felt as if the whole valley had fallen silent.

I won't give up, though, vowed Little-Hare, his voice echoing in the new quiet. *I won't, I won't.*

He refused to be afraid, even though every fibre of his being instructed him to be terrified. He was determined to keep looking for the flower of hope, wherever he could find it.

He nudged open barn doors, and found spiders still spinning glittering web after web in the smoky corners. Cockroaches continued their restless foraging in the cellars, unabated. Pigeons, somehow, still pecked about on the roof tops, squabbling among themselves as they had ever done.

The hares themselves seemed untouched, so far. They had been so close to Mooncalf, but they had always been careful too, as hares naturally are. It felt only a matter of time before their luck ran out.

That was another thing about the plague. All animals lived with fear as a constant on the edge of their lives, but now it became their central preoccupation.

The disease designed to terrify! sang the harvest mouse in a register that a human could only have described as operatic. *The one we call the berry-eye!*

*

Then, as Professor Jaynes had predicted, Facto at last

198

responded to his warnings on the virus.

One cold, clear morning in Badger Moon, Little-Hare and his sist-hare were about to settle back into their lonely forms, when he spied a large violet-coloured machine roar into the yard of Old Farm. It had a pointed front as sharp as any thorn, and black smoke poured from the rear. Even from the top of the hill, he could see the symbols on the side, the same symbols that had been on the professor's cabin, where he had been so cared for.

Come on, he said to Run-Hare. *They're friends of the professor's. He said Facto would come!*

The two hares ran down into the farm, peering from behind a barn corner as the door of the strange machine slid open. Some human men stepped out, who could not have looked less like farmers. They were all in black, wearing helmets, padded tops and trousers, with heavy boots on their feet and firesticks cradled in their arms. Their faces were masked as if the country air itself was poisoned. One walked with the aid of metal sticks. He appeared to be in charge.

Are you sure they're here to help? said Run-Hare.

I still have hope, said Little-Hare.

The man on metal sticks sniffed the air of the farmyard through his mask with suspicion, as he addressed the others. It was not in the animal tongue, but the hares managed to make out one sound, that the man repeated many times.

Culling.

What does that mean, broth-hare? asked Run-Hare.

Perhaps they are going to all give us a cure, like the professor said?

Next, the man raised one of his metal sticks and a spout of flame shot into the air. It smoked and smelled. The hares edged further behind their barn door.

Little-Hare looked at his sist-hare.

I don't think this is a cure. Not the one I was expecting.

The men formed a line, and advanced towards the buildings and opens, but the hares were already running up the hill, and crying out to every animal who still lived and breathed in the valley, the warning that they all dreaded to hear –

Beast hunters!

The men in black first piled up the bodies of those beasts who had perished from the berry-eye, and then put a flame to them, clouds of black smoke billowing from vast bonfires into the sky. Next they began to cull, shooting any wild creatures who dared to live and were foolish enough to cross their path – and added their bodies to the burning pyres.

Little-Hare and Run-Hare hid in the long weeds, as they had not done since they were new and young in the world, a time when the world was but a jungle of green to them, when a fly crawling up a stem of green was a thing of wonder, and every tall-home seemed to touch the stars.

Now they watched as flames blazed where the sheep used to gather under the old oak. They saw men in masks pile bodies where he and Run-Hare used to joust. They turned away from indescribable horrors where the buzzard nearly picked him off by the marshes; and where Little-Hare had found a mooncalf on Miracle Moor, her mother silent beside her, blood once again stained the ground.

Not that the men cared. In fact, the men were too busy killing or burning to even notice the land they stood and slaughtered on.

The land that was still tinder-dry after a sweltering summer.

We should pull back, said Run-Hare from their hiding place. *We're not safe here.*

They then watched as a single spark danced through the air from one of the smouldering pyres on to the parched open. It set off a line of sparks, which crackled in the scorched, rain-starved green, catching on bone-dry leaves and weeds, which spread to longer grasses, then to Bristly Hedge, which tore a livid streak of fire right up the hill until it licked the horizon.

Little-Hare jolted upright. *The final omen from the bull's dream! Let the sun turn the sky bright with flames!*

It was here. The whole world was on fire. How quickly these things happened.

The fire scored black furrows along the open, sparks tumbling in the smoke, the green crackling with destruction, until the flames started to lick at the farm buildings themselves. Every word of the bull's dream had come true. A great wet, plague and wildfires.

The two hares ran and ran, faster than they'd ever run, powering into the wind. Little-Hare surged up the hill, scrambling for clean air as if he was coming up to the surface from underwater. He could feel the inferno's heat on his back, singeing the tips of his ears, and turning the sky black above his head.

The Terribleness was fully upon them, and if anything, it was more terrible than the bull had foretold. Blizzards, wets and drought had attacked their world, hard upon one another, like a pack of insatiable dogs. Then disease and fire had joined the hunt, and they had driven him hard.

The two hares climbed higher and higher away from the farm and the fire and the smoke, while the sun slowly dipped behind the distant horizon. They reached Bull's Bellow, once more their only refuge – for now.

*I understand now, sist-hare, * he said, as they tried to comfort one another.

What?

Fear. Everything else – the buzzard, the man capturing me, the great wet, even Dog—

– is nothing compared to this.

They drew closer still, as they could

hear the crackling from the valley, the
sharp bangs as machines exploded in the
heat, and every now and then, a sudden crash
as a tall-home toppled in the wood, streaming
with flame.

The whole world Little-Hare knew was on the
verge of disappearing for ever.

*How can we stop this, sist-hare? I should never
have been chosen! I'm too little, too young. I ran
away when I should have stayed, I left everything
too late—*

But through the wisps of smoke that drifted around
them, Run-Hare simply placed a paw on his mouth,
silencing him.

You forget our moth-hare, she said. *It is never
too late, chosen one.*

Little-Hare's eyes were watering, his throat dry
and itchy. He still felt the heat, unlike anything he
had ever known, blowing in his face. It was hard to
hear much over the crackle and the roar, but his hare
sense made him turn around.

There, behind him, in the ash-flecked crater of
Bull's Bellow, were others who had fled high and far
from the flames, just as the hares had. Not as many
as had marched on the farm, of course. But
enough. And as he turned his gaze away

from the inferno to the living creatures sheltering behind him, he finally realised what his fath-hare had meant after all.

The flower of hope. It grew *everywhere*, if only you knew where to look. It grew in the most lifeless hollowed-out craters, it grew in the bloodiest corners of slaughter barns, and it grew out of fiery conflagrations.

It always had.

Because it grew in him.

That was what Fath-hare had meant. Little-Hare had searched high and low, but he did not need to look any further. He stopped cowering, and felt himself straighten upright, vowing never to tremble in despair again. The flames below danced on the surface of his eye and he drew their power into him.

I am a finder of hope in a world of fear, he said slowly, *and I will not be stopped.*

I know, dear broth-hare.

One day, my Run-Hare, the wet will cease rising. I promise. The fires will burn no more, we will find a cure for this plague, the humans will stop slaughtering us, and the flower of hope will grow once more on these green slopes we call our home.

He looked down over the valley, the sparks of fire still smouldering in the gloom.

I just don't want to leave you alone.

Then there was a voice from behind him.

You're not leaving her alone, Little-Hare.

It was Stupid Chick. He stepped out from the crowd of surviving animals, followed by Lamb and Kid Goat.

Go on, then, scram. Or am I going to kick you out myself? said the robin. Little-Hare's friends gathered in a protective circle around his beloved sist-hare.

I'm going to warn every wild on the Island, he declared. *We can't save ourselves until we save everyone else too. I can't stop this plague, but I can still run, and warn others of what is to come. It is not too late for them to prepare.*

Waxwing called out from the dark. *Then why ARE YOU STILL HERE?*

And with a single leap, Little-Hare was gone, bounding off over the hills to deliver his message to the sleeping world, by the light of the silvery, miraculous moon.

A STORY BEGINS

Little-Hare finishes his story, but he does not tell them everything. There are some details which must be for this Wildness's ears only. They are too important, and he does not know if it is wise to share them with the whole of this wild. He has learned a thing or two, after all. He is about to ask the Wildness for a quiet word, when three wolves hurtle through the ferns into the circle, still roaring and fighting with each other.

You shouldn't have let him through!

*No, *you* let him through!*

We are sorry, your Wildness, says the eldest Guardian, the one with a developing grey muzzle. *This hare used his cunning to slip past us. Shall we deal with him for you?*

There follows an uneasy silence. Then the creature they

address tosses his horns and roars at them. He towers above them, a gigantic stag with a deep brown coat and a spreading crown of antlers on his head.

You are lucky I still allow you to be Guardians of this wild, he snaps. *This hare brings a message from the south of the Island that we cannot ignore.*

But, your Wildness, says the leader of the wolf pack, *he is but a hare—*

Indeed he is, and one with more bravery and wisdom in one ear than the unfortunates I see arranged before me. We are in grave danger. Prepare our wild for travel, immediately.

The wolves are in uproar. *Travel? We like it here, your Wildness.*

I'm not going anywhere till I've had my dinner, says another, eyeing the hare.

The stag sighs. *I shall not repeat myself.* He glances at them. *Or do you want to feel the sharp end of my antlers?*

Without another word, the wolves turn on their heels and begin rounding up the wild who had stood around the stag and Little-Hare. They had been hanging on his every word, and now they prepare to leave the wood that has been their home for as long as they can remember. Deer with furry red-brown backs, badgers blinking in the late afternoon light and snowy mountain hares, all of them begin gathering their young, taking what food they can.

If he squints and looks up at the white circle of sky in the oak canopy above, Little-Hare can see a flock of grey pigeons filling the sky. They are joined by rooks, jackdaws and even bats, unhooking themselves early from their roosts.

Seemingly out of nowhere, butterflies, bees and dragonflies appear in busy clouds. Ants march from under logs, and a bossy cockroach marshals his troops over a rock. Among the crowd, he thinks he spies a wildcat, a slithering adder, even a pine marten or two.

A whole forest is on the move.

For a moment, Little-Hare feels free. All the hunger, pain, exhaustion and fear – it is like he steps out of them, shedding a skin he has worn for too long. He has completed his journey and delivered his message.

Where will you go? he asks the stag.

The deer does not reply at first. He is sniffing the air, staring into the horizon at something the hare cannot see. *As far north as we can, as far away from the winds that blow this berry-eye after us. To the sea itself, if we must.*

And then?

We wait. I have heard there is a place there where not even humans venture. We will be out of sight, out of mind, safe for a while.

Little-Hare nods, silent, trying to ignore the bursting heart within him, the heart that wants to join the journey north with all its might.

You can come with us, you know, says the stag.

211

Little-Hare shakes his head.

No. I've already endangered you by coming here. By some miracle, I have escaped it for now . . .

You fear for your sist-hare.

The Terribleness was still spreading when I left. It is so quick . . .

And if the worst happens?

Then we will make one last journey to a Forest of the Dead and pass our final days there.

Little-Hare studies his reflection in a puddle by the speaking rock he has been perched on. It is hard to tell if that is light from the setting sun, or a red tinge to his eye – he looks away. No. Not now.

He's not ready yet. There's one last thing he has to do.

As I travelled here, I heard rumours. Of your bravery and courage. You are the greatest and mightiest wild beast in the whole Island.

You don't need to flatter me, hare.

But I need to be sure you can do what I'm going to ask.

Now the stag fixes him with his gaze. *The human.*

Little-Hare nods. *He is the only one we can trust. The one who can talk to animals. Jaynes. He promised us a cure. That is the only way we will ever be free again.*

Stag digests this information for a moment. *Then, we must find that human too. His magic could save us all.*

You give me your word?

You have my word! I have spies in the sky, soldiers underground, Guardians faster than the wind. There is much a wild can still do, away from humans.

Little-Hare nods. Then he jumps off the rock, picking up his scent for the journey back through the stag wood, out and off on to the moors. He takes a deep draught of water from the puddle under the boulder, and a large mouthful of green to get him off to a good start. He stretches, and takes one last look at the ancient forest, and the beast who is nature's last stand against the plague.

You're very brave for a hare, you know, says the stag, a kindness to his voice that Little-Hare had not noticed before.

But his whiskers and ears shake the compliment away.

He gazes ahead at the gathering darkness

of the forest, emptying of life as its inhabitants prepare for the journey of their lives. They are fleeing danger, and he is returning to the heart of it.

He studies his paws.

No, Stag, I'm not brave. I'm like all hares. Watchful, timid, the first to run, the last to act.

Then how did you make it here, through everything you've seen, all that destruction, the death, the horror?

For the same reason that you're going to find that cure and stop this plague. He prepares to run. *Something that no plague will ever take away from us. The flower of hope, Stag. I made it here for that alone. Let it grow.*

Then he dives into the bracken without another word, scuttering towards home, but the stag has heard all he needs to hear. He will take the hare's precious flower and store it deep inside his heart, for he will have need of it in the days that follow, more need than he can yet imagine.

He turns his head towards the sun slipping through the bare trees, as he bellows for his wild and the journey to come. There is new life stirring in the ground beneath his feet. This glade will soon be covered in fresh snowdrops, as it always is. A bright, pale bullfinch sounds her doleful call in the slender branches of the rowan above his head, signalling the end of one year, the beginning of another.

A new year, a new story.

IT HAS
ONLY JUST
BEGUN ...

In parks and in forests, in gardens and on balconies,
in fields and between cracks in the pavement . . .
there is wildness to be found everywhere!
Taking inspiration from the illustrations in this book,

YOUR MAP HERE!

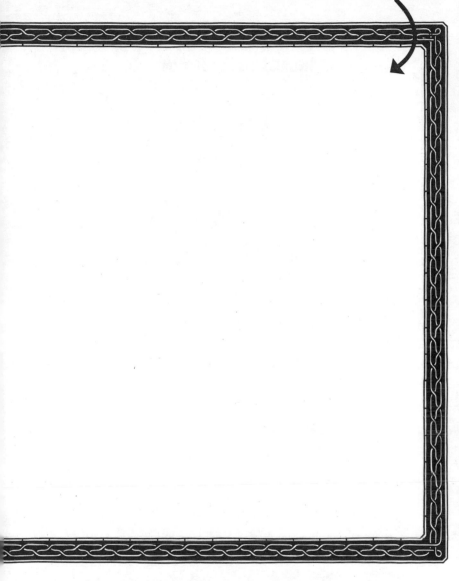

can you make a map of your nearest wild space?
A grown-up could help you to share a photo of it with
the author using the contact details on his website:
www.pierstorday.co.uk/contact

DON'T MISS KESTER JAYNES'S
INCREDIBLE STORY IN

THE
LAST
WILD

READ A SNEAK PEEK FROM
THE FIRST CHAPTER . . .

I used to be able to talk normal, you see, like everyone. Mum and I talked a lot. Dad and I talked a bit. Now though, it's like trying to learn the hardest language in the world. I know I can inside; it's just when I try to speak – nothing happens. The more I try, the harder it gets.

They want to make me talk again here – Doctor Fredericks with his tests – but it's not working. People still stare at you funny as you go red in the face, or sometimes they laugh and make up what they think you were going to say.

I'd rather try and talk to a varmint, thanks. There's enough of them – that's for sure. Flapping moths that circle round lights, like the one in my room right now, and spiders lurking in corners, or cockroaches scuttling around by the bins. All the useless insects and pests that the red-eye left behind. We don't even bother with their real names half the time. Varmints is all they are.

And I have practised talking at them, as it happens. Not that you're meant to go near them – even though everyone knows they're the only thing that can't get the virus. So I haven't reported this flapping one in my room.

Because I like practising with him there buzzing around. He won't talk back. But at least he doesn't laugh or stare – I can almost pretend he's listening.

I do that a lot.

Right, varmint, I say to myself in my head, *let's see what you think I'm saying this time.*

So I'm just about to have a go at saying 'B-E-D' again – or at least the 'B', or even a noise that sounds like a 'B' – when the speaker hidden in the ceiling splutters into life. You can almost see the spit fly out of the holes. The varmint whirls angrily away; he doesn't like it any more than I do.

'Calling all, ah, students. Your first meal of the day is, ah, served, in the Yard. You have t-t-ten minutes.'

There's a clank as he replaces the microphone in its stand, and a hum as he forgets to turn it off and I hear his heavy breathing for a minute before he remembers and flicks the switch.

Doctor Fredericks, the Governor.

He can give himself as many titles as he likes; he's still just an ugly man in a white coat with a comb-over, whose breath smells of sweets. The day after they brought me here – bundled out of my home in the middle of the night – I gathered with all the new kids in the Yard while he stood behind a lectern reading words off a screen, his jacket flapping in the air-con.

'Good afternoon, ahm, boys and, er, girls. Welcome to S-Spectrum, ah, Hall. You have been sent here because your parents want to, ahm, f-f-forget about you. Your, ah, schools can no longer t-t-tolerate you, so they have asked us to help. Because we are a special institution, dealing with special c-c-cases like yours. And I'll tell you now how it's going to, ahm, work.' His amplified words bounced off the walls. 'Look behind you at the sea. It is the filthiest and most p-p-polluted sea in the world, we're told.'

He stared down at us through his bottle-top glasses and flicked away a loose strand of greasy hair as we gazed out of the glass walls behind us at the waves chopping and crashing at the cliffs.

But I didn't believe that Dad wanted to forget about me.

Six years later, I still don't.

'There are t-t-two ways, ah, out of here. Through our front gates, as an improved and functioning member of society. Or off these bally c-c-cliffs and into the, ahm, sea. So either learn to, ah, m-m-modify your behaviour, or jolly well learn to, ah, dive!'

I haven't learnt to do either yet.

I pull on my trackies, shove my feet into my trainers and strap on my watch. Then there's a beep, and the light in my door goes red, orange, then green, before sliding open with a hiss. The fat warden is standing there in his crumpled purple jacket and trousers, my door keycard dangling on a strap from around his wrist.

'Come on, Jaynes,' he mutters, scratching his hairy chin. 'I haven't got all day.'

I'm not surprised, with so much sitting on your bum and sleeping to do, I think. That's one of the advantages of not being able to speak – you never get in bother for talking back. I step out into the corridor and wait.

One by one, the other doors along from me beep and slide open. And out come the other inhabitants of Corridor 7, boys and girls my age, all in trackies and trainers like me, their hair unbrushed, their faces blank. We look at each other, and then the warden silently points to the other end of the corridor.

I feel his eyes boring into my back as we walk past him along the passage and into the open lift.

The Yard is full of noise, which gets right inside my head. Most of it from the queue for the servery, a polished counter set into the wall, lined with pots. Metal pots full of pink slop, which some women with grey hair and greyer faces are busy dishing out, all of them wearing purple tunics with a big F stamped on the front.

F for Factorium. The world's biggest food company. More like the only food company now, since the red-eye came and killed all the animals. Every last one, apart from the varmints.

So Facto started making formula for us to eat instead. Which now makes them the only *company*, full stop – they run *everything*. First the government asked them to take care of the red-eye, and then they ended up taking care of the government. They run the country now, from hospitals to schools. Including this one. I don't know why making food or killing animals makes you good at running schools as well, but the first thing you learn in a Facto school is: never argue with Facto.

'What's the flavour, miss?' shouts Wavy J, waving his plastic bowl in the air, somehow first in the queue already. That's why he's called Wavy – he's always at the front of every line, waving. I don't even know his real name.

Behind him is Big Brenda, a fat girl with hair in bunches who has to sleep on a reinforced bed. She's here because she ate her mum and dad out of house and home – even during the food shortage – and got so big they couldn't look after her any more. That pale-faced kid with bags under his eyes is Tony – who got in trouble for stealing tins of food. And now he's here, quietly nicking some headphones out of the bag belonging to Justine, who is here because she was caught being part of a gang. A gang of thieves who got around everywhere on bikes, who nicked not just tins of food, but anything they could get their hands on. Like music players and headphones. That little kid she's talking to with spiky hair and a devil grin – that's Maze, who has an attention deficiency. The kind of attention deficiency that makes you chase your mum around the kitchen with a knife. And then right at the back, behind them all, is me.

I know their names. I listen to their conversations. I know why they're here.

But I don't know why I am.

ACKNOWLEDGEMENTS

I was inspired to return to the world of the wild by Greta Thunberg, who has moved the dial on the global climate change conversation to another level, and I pay tribute to her clear-sighted focus on speaking truth to power and her inspirational speeches to children across the world.

Publishing a book about a pandemic breaking out while a pandemic *actually* breaks out has been no mean feat. I am indebted to my agent Clare Conville for her persistent faith and relentless determination. I am also grateful to Quercus Children's and the Hachette Children's Group for their constant and deep support at a challenging time in the trade, in particular my editor Sarah Lambert and her cover Katherine Agar.

If you are reading this book, or thinking about reading this book, you may well have only heard about it thanks to the incredible promotional efforts of Emily Thomas, Lucy Clayton, James McParland and Katy Cattell at HCG, and Hannah Macmillan, Jason Bartholomew and the team at Midas PR.

I am enormously grateful that Thomas Flintham has also returned to the world of the wild, with another astonishing cover, map and pages of beautiful artwork, all designed and laid out by the genius that is Samuel Perrett.

A huge thanks also to my production editor Aliyana Hirji, copyeditor Jenny Glencross and proofreader Belinda Jones, for guiding these hares safely over hill and dale in the final stages of their journey, with so much thoughtful care and attention to detail.

Many other writers' work were invaluable in inspiring and informing my own. Marianne Taylor taught me all there is to know about hares in *The Way of the Hare*. During lockdown, some wonderful nature writers brought the British countryside into my London home. Those who really got me down amongst the weeds looking up at the stars were John Lewis-Stempel and his excellent books on hares in the fields today, *The Running Hare* and *The Private Life of the Hare*, Stephen Moss's diary of a rural year, *Wild Hares and Hummingbirds*, and Catherine Hyde's gorgeous, lyrical *The Hare and Moon*. In this fantastical, allegorical world of talking animals, any real-life natural history I learned from them, but the inventions, contradictions and elaborations are all mine.

We have been spread far and wide from those we know and love, locked down and locked out. Thank goodness for the nourishing, joyful and generous friendship of my fellow children's writers, in particular Abi Elphinstone, Lauren St. John and Katherine Rundell.

Most of all, I would like to thank my husband Will, who has had little choice over the last year to live with this book more than anyone could reasonably expect. He is my first reader, my first editor, and I simply couldn't do this without him.

Photo © James Betts

Piers Torday began his career in theatre and then television as a producer and writer. His first book for children, *The Last Wild*, was shortlisted for the Waterstones Children's Book Award and nominated for the CILIP Carnegie Medal. His second book, *The Dark Wild*, won the Guardian Children's Fiction Prize. *There May Be a Castle*, published in 2016, received widespread critical acclaim and was a Children's Book of the Year for *The Times*. *The Lost Magician*, published in 2018, was a Book of the Year in six national newspapers. Piers has also completed an unfinished novel by his late father Paul Torday (author of *Salmon Fishing in the Yemen*), *The Death of an Owl*, and adapted *The Box of Delights* and *A Christmas Carol* for the stage.

LOOK OUT FOR MORE
ENTHRALLING ADVENTURES
BY PIERS TORDAY . . .

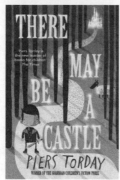

COLLECT THEM ALL!